A
Harlequin
Romance

OTHER
Harlequin Romances
by MARY BURCHELL

Many of these titles are available at your local bookseller, or through the Harlequin Reader Service.

For a free catalogue listing all available Harlequin Romances, send your name and address to:

HARLEQUIN READER SERVICE,
M.P.O. Box 707, Niagara Falls, N.Y. 14302
Canadian address: Stratford, Ontario, Canada.

or use order coupon at back of book.

PAY ME TOMORROW

by

MARY BURCHELL

HARLEQUIN BOOKS   TORONTO
WINNIPEG

Original hard cover edition published
by Mills & Boon Limited.

This edition © Mary Burchell 1974

SBN 373-01792-8

Harlequin edition published June 1974

Printed in Canada

1792

CHAPTER ONE

Susan Laverhope paused in the doorway, surveying the scene before her. In all her thirteen years she had never had the pleasure of making such a sensational announcement as the one which now trembled on her lips, and she intended to enjoy the moment to the full.

She looked at Ismay's beautiful fair head, bent slightly over the needlework she was doing, at Adrian idling in the window-seat with that air of picturesque grace common to all the Laverhopes, at Avril absorbed in one of her silly old books on art. Then, drawing a deep breath, she announced :

'Aunt Georgina's dead.'

The effect was instantaneous and gratifying.

'Aunt Georgina !'

'How do you know?'

'It isn't possible !'

'Of course it's possible.' Susan was not going to have her moment spoilt by base incredulity. 'Everybody's got to die some time and——'

'Not the Aunt Georginas of this world. They're immortal.' That was Adrian, who always said slightly shocking things with a specially languid air.

'That's blasphemy, I should think, now she's dead,' Susan remarked. 'Isn't it, Ismay?' She came and stood close beside her elder sister.

'No.' Ismay was comfortingly positive. 'But how did you know about Aunt Georgina? Who told you?'

'Nobody told me. I just happened to be in the hall when the phone rang, and Father answered. It must have been a telegram, because I heard him say, "'Miss Georgina Eltham died suddenly this morning'? Thank you." Just like that.'

'I don't call it sudden to die at ninety-one,' commented Avril, fixing great thoughtful grey eyes on her young sister. 'And you've got a ladder in your tights,' she added with characteristic irrelevance. Avril could look more beautifully attentive than all the rest of the family put together, but more likely than not her thoughts would be on something entirely removed from the subject of conversation.

'Have I? Oh, gosh!' Susan twisted round to survey the backs of her legs as well as she could. 'That's the third pair this week. I never knew any single person so unlucky with tights as I am. Why, Carol Elthorpe says her mother buys her six pairs for her birthday and six pairs for Christmas, and would you believe it, she makes them last for——'

'Never mind, my child,' her brother interrupted her once more. 'Do you realise that you can now have enough tights to tie knots round Carol Elthorpe—whoever she may be? We're all of us rich for the first time in our lives. No longer will the "lovely Laverhopes" have to wear laddered tights or draw lots for who shall charm the butcher into extending our credit a little further. Aunt Georgina has done her duty by the family at last and—in Roberts's affecting phrase—has passed away. We are—or, rather, Father is—the richer by something like a hundred thousand pounds. Life is about to begin.'

'You ought not to talk like that, Adrian,' Ismay protested. 'It's not—not decent.'

6

'You ought to go on the stage,' commented Susan. 'You've just the same silly ways as Father.'

'Susan!' exclaimed both her sisters in horror, for the legend of Father's brief stage career was something much more sacred than the death of Aunt Georgina.

Susan looked faintly—but only faintly—abashed.

'Well, I—I didn't mean that quite. I mean, you *expect* Father to be all melodramatic and to make speeches since he is—was—an actor. But Adrian needn't.'

Before Adrian could challenge this, however, the door opened once more and their father came into the room, slowly and with a gravity which he—and possibly even they—felt befitted the occasion.

Even at fifty-five, Laurence Laverhope still retained something of the fantastic good looks which had made him a matinée idol for a brief season in his youth. All too soon an infatuated public had reluctantly realised that, while good looks are a pleasant addition to, they are not a sufficient substitute for, the power to act. At least, not in an actor.

He still retained, however, the charm and the beautifully pitched voice which all his children had inherited. He also retained the certainty that an admiring audience waited on his every word, and, as he looked round now with an air of reflective melancholy, he might have been about to deliver Buckingham's speech to the populace on his way to execution.

What he did say was not quite so impressive.

'Children, you will be very grieved to hear that your Great-aunt Georgina died in her sleep at four-thirty this morning.'

No one—not even Susan—thought of spoiling Father's

announcement by telling him that this news was already known to them. And after the faintest pause he continued :

'This is hardly the moment to remember that we were not always perhaps quite in agreement with your great-aunt. She had her faults. We no doubt have ours.' Everyone knew this was a graceful gesture rather than a sincere belief. 'But death is a great leveller. There is no need to remember more now than that she was that rarity in the world today—a great lady.'

No one—not even Adrian—thought of interrupting this obituary notice, the eloquence of which evidently gave Father genuine pleasure. They looked becomingly grave and attentive.

Then Susan, unable to contain herself any longer, inquired with indecent cheerfulness :

'Shall we go and live at Estercourt now?'

This followed rather badly on Father's reference to a great lady, and even Ismay felt that Susan had invited the glance of pained astonishment which Father bent upon her.

'My dear,' he said in the accepted stage tone for a parent rebuking an erring child, 'your great-aunt has not been dead twelve hours. Is it for us to begin parting her possessions among us at this time?'

No one seemed to have an answer to this, presumably, rhetorical question, and in the ensuing silence Father made a very telling exit.

When he was well out of hearing Susan pouted and protested indignantly :

'Nobody said anything about parting possessions. I wish Father wouldn't always talk like Shakespeare or the least

8

interesting bits of the Bible.'

'You do Shakespeare less than justice, my dear,' Adrian assured her. 'But, anyway, I shouldn't worry about Father's rebuke if I were you. No one is more frantically relieved than he at the turn events have taken.'

'Adrian, it isn't specially witty to say those things,' Ismay reminded him sharply. 'And you certainly shouldn't say them to Susan.'

'Why not to me?' Susan wanted to know, while Adrian gave a smiling little shrug.

'I'm sorry, darling. But the truth *is* the truth, however regrettable. No one can suppose that a man in Father's position could remain inconsolable for the death of a most unlikeable old lady, when the consolation comes in the form of a desperately needed fortune. Why, he must have an overdraft as long as my arm, and practically no idea where the next penny is coming from.'

'What's an overdraft?' inquired Susan, ghoulishly interested in this description of her father. But no one told her because at that moment Avril suddenly spoke with that dreamy determination of hers which always commanded attention.

'I know *exactly* what I'm going to do. I've often lain awake at night thinking what I should do when the money did come. I shall go to Italy and study art all day long and paint and paint and paint. I shall go to Rome, to the best teachers there. And when I'm not working I shall wander round Italy. To Verona and Lake Garda, to Florence and Vallombrosa. I shall watch the Arno rushing under the arches of the Ponte Vecchio, and the line of the cypress trees against the evening sky, and the lizards running in the sun on the old stone walls. And I'll forget there was ever such a thing as fog or rain or cold.'

'It sounds heavenly,' Ismay agreed.

'You'll have snow in Rome during the winter,' Adrian warned her prosaically, but he too smiled at the picture Avril conjured up.

'I wish someone would tell me what an overdraft is,' persisted Susan.

'There's the romantic temperament for you,' declared Adrian, with mock despair. 'Here are we enthusing about the glories of Italy, and all the child can babble about is an overdraft.'

'Well, one ought to *know* these things. They may be useful one day. What is it, anyway?'

Adrian looked at her very seriously and said :

'An overdraft is something you're always asking your bank manager to let you have, and when you've got it you spend the time wondering how the deuce you can get rid of it.'

The two older girls laughed, but Susan said witheringly:

'I don't see that that makes sense.'

'It doesn't,' Adrian assured her. 'Nor do most other things with no money attached, come to that.'

'Well, anyway, we have plenty of money now,' Avril put in impatiently. And, getting up, she strolled gracefully out of the room with an air of already being about to begin the preparations for her journey.

Adrian looked after her thoughtfully. Then he smiled and stretched his arms above his head.

'Yes, we've plenty of money at last. Think of it ! Medical school for me. I know I could get a grant—but can any of you see me existing on a grant? Now I can do it in reasonable comfort. And then one day, poppet,' he assured

Susan, 'you'll be proud to point out your brother as one of the leading doctors of the day.'

'I shouldn't like to have you for a doctor,' Susan retorted. 'You haven't enough sense of responsibility.'

'Never mind, Adrian, you'll have a beautiful bedside manner,' Ismay told him, with a smile.

But Adrian turned on her at that, in sudden, unusual anger.

'Damn the bedside manner! That isn't what I want. Don't you see that's all this family has ever been any good for? Picturesque—charming—handsome—the lovely Laverhopes! I hate it all, every word of it. We're cursed with the power of looking decorative in every single situation. How did Father ever get on to the stage?—Because he was a sight to fill every stall with a fluttering female. And why wasn't he able to stay there?—Because he hadn't the plain wits or common sense to learn his job. I want to be a doctor—not a blue-eyed heart-throb. I'm sick to death of everyone saying what a wonderful-looking family we are. I sometimes almost wish I had a squint.'

'It'd be very inconvenient,' Susan pointed out. 'And weaken your sight too.'

'Oh, Adrian dear, I'm sorry.' Ismay patted her brother's arm sympathetically. 'I know what you mean. And I daresay it's specially rotten for a boy. I sometimes think you have a good deal of Mother in you.'

'I have?' Adrian gave a short laugh—a little ashamed of his outburst now. 'Oh no. I can remember her quite well. You're the only one of us who is the least like her. It's something to do with patience and having a charitable sense of humour, I think.'

Ismay laughed a little and coloured slightly.

'I'm not at all like her to look at,' she said.

'No, of course not. You're much more beautiful. When you come to think of it, Mother must have found it funny being the only ordinary-looking person in a family of beauties.'

'I think,' Ismay said, 'that was just what she found it— funny. It was one of the nicest things about her.'

'I expect you're right.' Adrian's casual good humour was entirely restored as he went off 'to make sure,' as he said, 'that the obituary notice to *The Times* displayed only Father's less embarrassing clichés.'

When he had gone Susan turned back to her elder sister.

'Well, if Avril's going to Italy and Adrian's going to college, what are you and I going to do?'

'I don't know.' Ismay smiled as she picked up her sewing again. 'What would you like to do?'

'Oh—lots of things.' Susan spoke with pleasurable vagueness. 'Is life really going to be very different, Ismay?'

'I—expect—so,' Ismay admitted slowly.

She was trying to imagine just how different it would be, for she could never remember a time when financial embarrassment had not been a daily companion. And yet somehow, on the insistence of Father, no one had ever done anything about it, except 'look decorative' as Adrian had said, and wait for Great-aunt Georgina to die.

The truth was that Laurence Laverhope was one of those men who ought never to have money left to them. Or rather, they should never know they are going to inherit it until the day when it actually becomes theirs. Great-aunt Georgina had been left a fabulously rich widow nearly half a century before, and had immediately announced that she intended her dear little nephew,

Laurence, to be her sole heir. She had been a delicate woman, disagreeably convinced that she was not long for this world, and therefore Laurence's parents had proceeded to bring him up with the pleasurable expectation that he would be a very rich man by the time he came of age.

In due course Laurence came of age, but his Aunt Georgina continued to enjoy her delicate health and her vast fortune.

With charming condescension he drifted on to the stage in order to fill in the time of waiting. After a while, a trifle bewildered, he drifted off again. Still Aunt Georgina's decease was delayed.

Then he married, for what was to prevent a man from marrying when he was (almost) in receipt of a very large income? While he still waited for the income to materialise he somehow contrived to live and bring up a family on a small private income left by his father, a great deal of credit, and the firm belief that, if he were not exactly a very rich man, he was at least only one stage removed from it.

No one had ever heard his wife express an opinion on the golden future in store for them. It was possible, of course, that she was much too busy making what she could of the far from golden present. Four children, however beautiful, had to be fed and clothed and looked after, and their wants certainly would not wait for the time when Great-aunt Georgina should die and leave them a fortune, whether it were this year, next year, some time or—horrid thought!—never.

In the end Laurence Laverhope's wife died ten years before Great-aunt Georgina, and, because she was amused by her family as well as loving them dearly, it is possible that her last sensation was one of humorous regret that she would never see how they did react when the long-awaited fortune became theirs.

Some such thought was in Ismay's mind now because—Adrian was right—she was the nearest in disposition to their dead mother.

'Mother would have been terribly amused if she could have seen us now,' she said aloud, hardly noticing that her young sister was still there beside her.

'Why? It's nice being left a fortune, but not exactly funny.'

'N-no, not funny. But I think she would have been intrigued to see how we all reacted, now that it's come at last. I don't think she ever quite believed in it herself.'

'I didn't either,' Susan confessed. 'Great-aunt Georgina was so jolly careful not to give us anything when she was alive that I can't imagine her being dead will alter anything much. Why, even that one time she gave Adrian half a crown for being third in class she took back a shilling when she found there were only four in the class. It doesn't seem to go with leaving a fortune to *any*one, somehow.'

Ismay smiled.

'I know. I sometimes felt a bit that way too. Only Father always talked as though everything in the world could wait until we were rich, and after a while, so much depended on it that I simply couldn't believe the fortune wasn't waiting just round the corner.'

'Well, so it was,' Susan pointed out practically.

'Yes, I know.' Ismay saw no reason to harrow her sister now with an account of how near to disaster they had been, but she knew—better perhaps than anyone else —the sea of debt and confusion that would have engulfed her father if Great-aunt Georgina had chosen to die even at ninety-two instead of at ninety-one.

'Do you think Avril will really go to Italy to study art?' Susan's thoughts had gone off on another tack now.

'Yes, I expect so. She nearly always does exactly what she means to.'

Susan nodded.

'I think she had some idea of how she was going to do it even if Great-aunt Georgina *hadn't* died,' she said.

Ismay glanced up in surprise.

'Oh, but she couldn't have managed it. There was no possible way of doing it without money, and I know Father hadn't a penny to spare for anything extra.'

'Oh, I don't think it was anything to do with Father. I think it was something not quite—well, something she thought we shouldn't like, because she said "art excused a lot of things," or something silly like that.'

'Did she?' Ismay looked disturbed. She knew that of all the family Avril was much the most incalculable. 'I don't expect she was speaking very seriously, Susan?' It was more a question than a reassuring statement.

'She *looked* serious,' Susan insisted. 'In fact, she looked jolly mad, because she was just leading off rather about not having any money of her own. I think perhaps it had something to do with Mr. Otterbury.'

'Mr. Otterbury! But she hardly knows him. He couldn't possibly have anything to do with her going to Italy.'

'Well, perhaps I'm wrong.' Susan glanced at that possibility with reluctance. 'But I'm pretty sure he had something to do with it. He did dance with her at the County

15

Ball, remember. And he offered to let her ride one of his horses if she wanted to.'

'Yes, I know. And Father put his foot down pretty firmly,' retorted Ismay, setting her soft mouth very firmly.

'*Why* wouldn't Father let her go riding, Ismay? At least, I mean—why wouldn't he let her borrow one of Mr. Otterbury's horses?'

'Because one doesn't put oneself under an obligation to men like Mr. Otterbury.' Ismay's tone was positive, but it only served to interest Susan further.

'Father said he was "a wrong 'un". What does that mean exactly?'

'Oh—well, it's Father's way of saying he isn't the kind of person he would like us to know.'

'Is that all?' Susan was disappointed. But Ismay added nothing to her explanation. Nor did she question her young sister further. If there were anything more to be asked she would ask Avril direct.

She glanced at Susan now and thought, with a slight sigh, that though she and Avril were almost identical in colouring—with the cloudy grey eyes and the real red-gold hair—they were entirely different in temperament. Susan was a downright, inquisitive, sometimes tiresome but always understandable schoolchild. Avril was remote, even secretive, queerly independent of other people, frankly self-centred, but with strange flashes of charm that could make up for weeks of indifference.

Ismay loved them both—as indeed she loved all her family—but there was no denying that Susan was a much simpler problem than the twenty-year-old Avril.

Adrian, for all his assumed air of nonchalance, was more like Ismay herself, both in looks and in tempera-

16

ment. They both had the same dark blue eyes and corn-coloured hair as their father. But they had inherited their balanced sense of values from their mother, and were united by a sense of humour which was singularly lacking in the other members of the family. Adrian's sense of humour was perhaps keener than Ismay's—certainly his sense of the ridiculous was—but it was also a good deal less kind. And while Ismay's smile had never made anyone feel uncomfortable, Adrian's most certainly had.

When Susan had finally gone about some faintly mysterious business of her own, Ismay folded up her sewing and went upstairs to the room which she shared with Avril. She had rather expected to find her sister dreaming by the window—a favourite occupation of hers—but instead she was in a fever of occupation.

Both doors of the huge old wardrobe which they shared stood open, and everything which Avril possessed had been taken out and thrown on her bed for a hurried but critical inspection.

'What on earth——?' began Ismay. But Avril interrupted her.

'There's not a single thing that will do. Isn't it marvellous? Father will have to re-equip me from top to toe. I *might* take that'—she scornfully twitched the skirt of a grey angora frock—'I suppose I shall need one warm thing. But I can't really connect anything else I have with going to Italy.'

Ismay sat down on the other bed and laughed.

'Are you starting off tomorrow?'

'Um?' Avril smiled slightly too. 'No. But I love getting everything worked out in my mind first. It's half the fun.'

'You *had* it all worked out, hadn't you, Avril? Even

17

before Aunt Georgina died, I mean.'

'Yes. Why not?' Avril's eyes were on the clothes again, and the faintest cool touch of remoteness had crept into her tone. It was not quite like a door being closed—more like the drawing of a thin curtain.

'It was counting your chickens a good while before they were hatched, for all you knew.'

'Well, we all did that all our lives, didn't we?' Avril's voice was too soft to be defiant, but a breath of resentment was perceptible.

'Yes. Too much so, I daresay. But this was something much more definite. You weren't only thinking of Great-aunt Georgina, were you?'

Avril raised her head quickly and, seeing the queerly innocent look in those cloudy grey eyes, Ismay had the peculiar impression that a lie was coming. Speaking hastily, before Avril could, she challenged her bluntly.

'Susan says you had some idea that Keith Otterbury would help you.'

There was a second's pause. The thin curtain had become a thick curtain.

'Did she?'

'Avril, you *couldn't* have had any idea of letting *him* take a hand in our affairs?'

'*My* affairs.'

'But, my dear, what was your idea? How do you suppose he could have helped you?'

'With money, of course. It's the only way anyone can help. Surely we've had that shown clearly enough all our lives?'

'But—*his* money? Avril, do you know what you're talking about? You couldn't seriously have thought of taking

18

money from a man like Keith Otterbury? Had he offered it, anyway? How did you even come to discuss such a thing?' Ismay was terribly distressed and made no attempt to hide the fact.

Avril shrugged slightly, and, picking up a flowered terylene frock, she held it against herself and studied her reflection in the mirror.

'Well, it doesn't matter now, anyway, does it? Because we're rich and I don't have to think about anyone helping me.'

'But'—Ismay bit her lip—'I don't think you can dismiss it like that.'

'I *have* dismissed it like that,' Avril said, and she gave her perfectly heavenly smile.

Ismay came over to her, took the dress away from her, and tossed it on the bed again. Then she caught both Avril's hands.

'Look here, Avril, have you been seeing a good deal of him? Father would have a fit if he knew. And anyway Keith Otterbury isn't the kind of person one—one makes a friend of.'

'I wasn't going to make a friend of him.'

'Then *what*? Do be a bit more frank, Avril. I could shake you.'

'Well then, if Great-aunt Georgina hadn't providentially died, I should have gone with Keith Otterbury to Italy. He travels a lot, you know—and always in such comfort.'

Ismay fell back from her.

'You were *going away* with him? Do you mean——'

'The usual thing? Of course.'

'Avril, I feel I don't know you, even after all these years,

19

when you talk like that. How can you possibly stand there calmly telling me you're going away with an absolute rotter just because he'd got more money than he knows what to do with?'

'But I'm not going, darling. That's the whole point. Great-aunt Georgina has prevented it—and I don't mind saying I'm glad.'

'But you *would* have gone. It's almost as bad as going. You speak as though there's nothing wrong in it—as though it's like—like going on the river for the day. If Great-aunt Georgina hadn't died——'

'But she *has* died, Ismay dear.' Avril laughed—a sweet laugh of genuine amusement. 'You're not a bit like the rest of us. You can agonise like anything over something that has never happened, while it's all we can do to give passing attention to a disaster that is almost upon us. You make such a lot of unnecessary anxiety for yourself.'

'No,' Ismay said. 'No, it's not anxiety—at least, not now that the danger is past. It's the shock of realising that you —that you could contemplate such a thing. It doesn't seem possible that one of·*us* could talk calmly of doing the sort of thing one only reads about.'

'But one doesn't only read about it.' It was Avril who sounded much the elder and more experienced now. 'You're awfully naïve in a way, Ismay. Funny—I believe you get it from Father, of all people,' she added irrelevantly. 'It's a plain fact that until today we had absolutely nothing but our looks to offer in the world market. I recognised the fact—even if you didn't—and I saw no reason to waste the one asset I had in the struggle to get what I wanted.'

'I think it's—frightful of you to talk like that.' Ismay

found that she was trembling slightly with something very much like anger.

'Well, darling, can't you comfort yourself with the fact that none of it ever happened?' Avril laughed, and actually gave Ismay a light, coaxing kiss. 'Can't you think of it as all hot air and bravado on my part?—something that I can talk about quite calmly because I should never really do it?'

Ismay looked at her doubtfully.

'Is that really it, I wonder?' she said with a sigh. And then, as Avril didn't answer—'That *was* it, wasn't it, Avril? You wouldn't really have done such a thing when it came to the point, would you? I wish you'd assure me of that.'

'Well, rest assured,' Avril told her lightly. But her smile had suddenly become a very secret smile again, as she turned to put away the despised dresses.

Ismay remembered that smile all day. And at night, when she lay awake, listening to the soft, untroubled breathing of her inexplicable sister, she felt almost as worried as if Avril still contemplated the crazy plan she had so coolly put forward.

That she should choose Keith Otterbury, of all people! Well, of course, he was the richest man in the county, and he had undoubtedly admired Avril at the County Ball, as Susan had said. But—he was an 'outsider'. (Funnily enough, all Father's slightly melodramatic terms of condemnation seemed to suit him.) Adrian always said that his name ought to be Sir Jasper, and that he ought to be seen philandering with a milkmaid in an ornamental smock.

He never had been seen doing any such thing, but there

was plenty of scandalous talk about him, all the same. The villagers classed all his escapades as 'goings-on in London', while the 'county' raised supercilious eyebrows and talked about the necessity of drawing the line somewhere. The line, it seemed, was drawn some way before Keith Otterbury.

It must be confessed that he himself remained peculiarly untroubled by either the scandalised state of the villagers or the superiority of the 'county'. He farmed his extensive estate admirably, he was considered a hard but fairly just landlord, and, while he was understood to take his pleasures where he found them when he was in town, when he returned to his estate, he certainly worked hard. Even his bailiff admitted that, and his bailiff, being an extremely efficient man himself, set a high standard.

'Oh well,' reflected Ismay uneasily, 'if Avril did want to weave some fantastic notion to herself, I suppose he was the obvious person to choose. I can't imagine anyone else in the district agreeing to take one of Father's daughters on a questionable trip abroad. But I wish she hadn't spoken so very much as though all the details had been arranged. I shouldn't think he is an easy man to lead on and then choke off. And if she really let him think she was that sort of girl——!'

Ismay decided that she would probably feel very angry and uncomfortable next time she met Keith Otterbury, riding his melodramatically black horse along the country lanes.

It was very wrong to feel glad that someone was dead, but, really, thank heaven Great-aunt Georgina had chosen just this moment!

The next few days were taken up with funeral arrangements suitable to the position of Great-aunt Georgina and the degree of awe which her family had felt towards her. No one—not even Father—could possibly pretend that deep affection prompted any of this. Great-aunt Georgina, after that one generous gesture of declaring that her nephew should be her heir, had never been known to do anything specially generous or kind again. She had been that most difficult of all tyrants, a gentle bully, and a reluctant submission to her sweetly stinging tongue had been the nearest thing to affection which her family had ever felt able to accord her.

There was a sense of relief, in more ways than one, in the Laverhope family just then. And it showed itself in various forms, from the mellifluous bass-baritone humming of Father, recalling ballads from his youth, to a disposition on Susan's part to disregard home lessons entirely.

'It seems silly, in a way, to be bothering *quite* so much about education when I shan't ever have to earn my own living,' she confided to Ismay.

Ismay, however, refused to see things quite in that light, and in this connection, at least, Great-aunt Georgina was invoked in vain.

The funeral was a stately affair, 'with Father in splendid form,' as Adrian whispered to Ismay. Ismay didn't smile, however. She was thinking how sad and futile it was that anyone should live in the world nearly a hundred years, and yet never discover the value of being loved instead of feared. The dreadful truth was that Great-aunt Georgina had never given greater pleasure in her life than she did by dying. 'And yet we're not a heartless family,' thought Ismay. 'At least—I suppose we're not.' And for a moment her eyes went to Avril, fair-skinned and exquisite in her simple black—bought on credit.

After the funeral only one person came back to the house with them, and that was a short, stocky man whom Ismay had noticed during the service because he was singularly impressive in spite of being almost completely bald.

'Who is he, Adrian?' she asked. 'I don't think I've ever seen him before.'

'No. He's the lawyer down from London. Going to read the will in style, I presume.'

'Read the will? But there isn't really much to read, surely?'

'I suppose not. But I don't think Father would want to be done out of a scene like that. I imagine we shall all sit round the dining-room table and look as though we don't know anything about what is going to be said. Then when the words are actually out, we shall permit ourselves an appearance of dignified pleasure, decently tinged with melancholy.'

'It seems rather silly.'

'It is, damned silly,' Adrian agreed. 'But I don't think that consideration ever stopped Father from doing anything in his life.'

Ismay made no reply, but she felt slightly silly and self-conscious when they were, as Adrian had prophesied, grouped round the dining-room table to hear the reading of the will. Susan—and Father—were probably the only people who were completely enjoying the scene, though Mr. Foster, the lawyer, permitted himself a certain grave geniality which, Ismay supposed, was the right expression to use when announcing good news to the heir of a client.

Mr. Foster broke the seal of the envelope he was hold-

24

ing, and drew out several sheets of paper.

'Great-aunt Georgina certainly took a lot of space to say she had left Father everything,' thought Ismay. 'I hope she hasn't included sarcastic advice to us all, along with it.'

Mr. Foster glanced round the table and cleared his throat.

'Before I read the will of the late Mrs. Eltham, I think I should say a few words. The will is a long one, with many and varied bequests, but I feel it will lessen the—ah —the anxiety and the—tension if I explain at once that every penny of Mrs. Eltham's money has been left to charity.'

CHAPTER TWO

THE scene which followed Mr. Foster's announcement had, for Ismay, very much the character of a nightmare. Afterwards she always had difficulty in recalling the lawyer's appearance, but she never forgot his voice.

The heavy drone of a bee invariably recalled to her the fantastic scene in the dining-room, where the family sat in stunned silence, while Mr. Foster's voice went on and on and on, reciting the list of charities to which Great-aunt Georgina had so generously left her fortune.

For a long time Ismay just stared at the tablecloth, noticing subconsciously how worn the pile was at the corners, and how lavishly spotted with ink in the place where Susan usually did her homework. Some of those blots were older still, dating from Avril's or Adrian's schooldays, or perhaps her own. 'One day' they had been going to have a new cloth, just as they had been going to have new furniture and new carpets and new clothes and a new life. One day—the day when Great-aunt Georgina's fortune passed to them at last.

Well, there was no such day. Great-aunt Georgina had died and her money had passed, not to them, but to all those excellent hospitals and institutions now being enumerated by Mr. Foster. Places which, no doubt, would make far better use of the money than the Laverhopes would ever have done. Perhaps it was right in a way. Only life had to go on, and just now life was a rather frightening matter.

26

At last Ismay raised her head and glanced, a little fearfully, at the faces round her.

Only Susan's retained any liveliness of expression, and she was listening with the greatest attention and curiosity to what Mr. Foster was saying. Perhaps she was fascinated by the sheer amount of the sums mentioned, or perhaps she had still not gathered that 'charity' did not include the family.

When Ismay's eyes came to Adrian, she felt her throat ache. For all his nonchalance and his deliberately frivolous manner, his heart, she knew, had been always set on his ambition to become a doctor. He had been sincere when he angrily repudiated any idea of enjoying the more spectacular side of the profession—he wanted to study and practise, to be something worthwhile and useful. And now —she could read the ruin of his hopes quite clearly in his white, set face, and the curiously bleak expression of his eyes. They were nice eyes—not only beautiful in colour, but with a curious sparkling warmth, and they could light very often with real generosity. Now they looked, somehow, blind.

Slowly her glance shifted to her father. He too was white, but he looked much more bewildered than Adrian. As yet he had not entirely grasped the situation, and there was something strangely pathetic about his instinctive effort to keep up general appearances while he groped bewilderedly for the cue to the part he should play. For once he had not been prepared. There was no precedent for this ghastly scene, no hint of the best way to handle it. There was something almost childlike in his distress. He was like a nice little boy who had trotted over to smell a rose and had his nose stung by a bee.

27

Ismay felt real pain as she looked at him, and quickly she glanced away to the last member of the family.

Avril, her chair tipped back slightly, was gazing thoughtfully out of the window at the clouds which drifted slowly across the sky. She was not paying the slightest attention to Mr. Foster. Indeed, she was entirely remote from the scene, and Ismay doubted if she were either hearing or seeing anything that was happening around her. Certainly any shock she might have felt had already passed. The situation was no longer useful to her —she had detached herself from it. With a cold little feeling of something like horror, Ismay thought :

'She's making other plans. Already she has gone back to her original idea. If she can't have what she wants in one way, then she means to have it in another. She is thinking of Keith Otterbury and his money—and his offer, whatever it was.'

It was over at last—this dreadful scene, with the implications which, even now, were hazy to them all. Mr. Foster gathered up his papers and became the man, rather than the lawyer, once more.

'I am very sorry,' he said. 'It would be idle to pretend this is not a very disappointing will, a very unkind will, one might say. But Mrs. Eltham was not a woman who was open to advice, still less to protest. There was nothing I could do about it.'

Father roused himself then. His public demanded that he should say something, and a little heavily he produced the suitable words.

'She was, of course, quite entitled to leave her money where she pleased. One must not allow disappointment to degenerate into bitterness.'

It was a very bitter little smile, however, that crossed Adrian's face.

'Aren't we going to have *anything*? Aren't we rich, after all, then?'

The crude candour of Susan's astonished demands made them all wince slightly. It was sad, but it was true. They were not rich, after all.

Somehow they got through the rest of that day. Mr. Foster tactfully intimated that urgent business in town necessitated his immediate return, and when he had gone, Father withdrew almost at once to the room which was known as his study. He never, of course, had done any study there—unless he studied the plentiful accumulation of bills which adorned his desk. But it was clearly understood that when he retired there he was not to be disturbed.

'Well,' Adrian said, 'there it is! The lovely Laverhopes face financial disaster—still looking decorative, but not knowing what the hell they're going to do.'

'Don't, Adrian.' Ismay glanced at him with something like pity. 'It doesn't help to be——'

'"Bitter" was Father's word,' Adrian reminded her savagely.

'Very well. Being bitter about it *doesn't* help.'

'Yes, but what *would* help?' Susan wanted to know. 'What can we do?'

'My dear,' Adrian told her, 'you have an unrivalled talent for asking those questions which one either cannot answer or which have only the most disagreeable answers to them.'

'Well, you needn't be a pig about it,' retorted Susan. '*I've* lost the money as well as you. And anyway, I only

29

asked. Even if you haven't got an answer, perhaps some-one else has. Ismay might. She's got lots more sense than you.'

Ismay put a restraining hand on her little sister's arm. It was awful enough that they should all be so disappointed and despairing. It would be ten times worse if they started bickering about it. Perhaps Adrian thought the same, because, with an effort, he restrained his irritation.

'All right, poppet, I'm sorry. Perhaps Ismay *has* got a solution. I'm afraid I haven't—short of my getting a job as a chemist's assistant, and the girls going to serve in a shop or to act as models. They're pretty enough, goodness knows.'

'I,' said Avril coolly, 'shall not serve in any shop, nor do I intend to be a model. The life has never appealed to me and never would.'

Adrian laughed shortly.

'You don't really think there's much choice confronting us, do you?'

'Oh—I don't know.' Avril's eyes looked deceptively dreamy. 'In actual fact we're no worse off than we were this time last week. We hadn't any more real money in our pockets then. I don't know why we should start running round in circles and talking despairingly now.'

'Don't you?' Adrian's tone was grim, though slightly amused. 'Because last week we were all living in a gorgeous, ridiculous, colossal dream. Now we've woken up. That's the difference. The central fact that has buoyed up our spirits and our credit all these years simply doesn't exist. We've been brought up to adorn riches one day.

Now riches refuse to adorn us. We're as decorative as ever —but we're poor. The two things don't go together. Nature abhors the combination a lot more than any vacuum.'

'Well, life doesn't begin and end with Great-aunt Georgina's will,' retorted Avril placidly. 'There *are* other things.'

'Such as?'

But Avril refused to be drawn.

Supper was a depressing meal, especially as Father refused to be tempted from the seclusion of his study. Not that he would have been specially cheerful company, but any meal seemed strange and incomplete without his slightly pompous, but not unkindly, presence.

'Doesn't Father want any supper?' Susan—her own appetite unaffected by grief—read in his absence a very serious state of affairs.

'No.' Ismay shook her head and looked worried. 'He asked for some sandwiches and coffee to be sent in.'

'And did you take them in? How did he look? Is he frightfully upset?' Susan was interested in securing a complete picture.

'I didn't go in.' Ismay hesitated a moment, and then added with a slight effort, 'The door was locked. He just called out to me to leave the tray on the table outside the door.'

'I say'—Susan paused suddenly with her fork half-way between her plate and her mouth—'you don't think he's going to commit suicide, do you? I mean, people *do* when they lose a lot of money.'

'You've been reading too much Dumas,' her brother

told her crushingly.

'No, I haven't. And anyway, why should he lock the door?'

'Because he probably remembers that's what the ruined hero does in all the best books. Retires with his grief behind locked doors. It's much better than to be so gross and insensitive as to come and enjoy a hearty meal in company with his family.'

'Do you think so?' Susan appealed to Ismay, rather than to her brother.

'Well, something like that, I dare say.' Ismay smiled. 'I don't think Father is in a suicidal mood, but he's probably very much upset and I expect he wouldn't like us to see him like that.'

'I—see. Shall I have to go and yell good-night through the door?'

'Perhaps he'll have come out by then,' Ismay suggested.

But he had not. Nor by the time that the others went to bed. Ismay lingered after Adrian and Avril had gone upstairs. She went round locking up and then hesitated again before putting out the lamp in the hall. Father was not a man who liked to be interrupted when he indicated a desire for solitude, but—he had been there alone too long. Suddenly making up her mind, Ismay went over and knocked on the study door.

'Who is that?' Father sounded tired and irritable.

'It's Ismay, Father.' She tried the door, but it was still locked.

'Oh—goodnight, my dear.'

'I want to come in, please. I want to speak to you.'

'Tomorrow. Go away now, my child.'

Ismay knew that if he addressed her as 'my child' he

was in one of his 'noble' moods, which usually meant that he was about to make an exceedingly foolish decision.

'No, please do let me in. The others have gone to bed, but I want to see you. You make me—nervous, refusing to see me like this.'

She heard her father get up from his chair then and, coming over, he unlocked the door and opened it. She was not sure whether he actually intended her to come into the room, but she brushed quickly past him and came into the circle of lamplight. Then, turning back to her father, who still stood by the door, she gave an exclamation of concern.

Poor Laurence Laverhope looked a very tired and wretched and disappointed man at that moment. All his life he had lived on pleasant hopes and a sense of well-being in which anticipation and reality were inextricably mingled. Now everything had faded and he looked—Ismay realised with dismay—an old man.

'What is it, my dear?' He spoke rather heavily.

'Only that—I don't like saying goodnight to you through the door.' She came and put her arm round him, smiling at him coaxingly though her eyes were anxious. 'Besides, I know you must be feeling simply awful, dear. It's such a dreadful disappointment—much worse for you than for any of us.'

Just for a moment the ex-matinée idol put his head down on his daughter's shoulder. It was a telling gesture, but it was perfectly sincere. He did indeed feel that everything was over and done with, and his desire for support was something almost physical.

Ismay rubbed her cheek affectionately against his hair. 'We'll manage all right. Things won't seem so bad when you've had a night's sleep. Why don't you go to bed now, with some hot milk and aspirin? And in the morning we'll talk things over together.'

'There's nothing to talk over, my dear. Nothing but bills.'

There was no striving after effect in that—nothing studiedly dramatic. It was just a stark fact discovered by a miserable and very frightened old man. Ismay found it far more moving than anything he had ever said. She kissed him warmly and spoke again with a cheerfulness she was far from feeling.

'Oh, you mustn't worry so much. Adrian and Avril and I will get jobs. We've never organised our lives very well before, but now we'll be sensible wage-earners, like thousands of other people. You've no idea how well we'll manage. And each month we'll set aside everything we can to pay the bills. Please, dear, go to bed now and don't wear yourself out worrying. It's going to be a big change for all of us, but there's no reason why we shouldn't make it a success.'

There wasn't very much logic in this, but the tone and the smile were encouraging. Finally he allowed himself to be persuaded. And when he kissed her forehead and remarked in his more usual, deep tone that 'no man had better daughters than he', Ismay felt sure he was feeling better. It was such a heartening return to his usual manner.

She took him up the aspirin and a glass of hot milk, and was moved to see his ingenuous pleasure at the attention. Really, there was something very childlike about Father. That was why you could never take him very seriously.

Afterwards, Ismay went downstairs again to his study,

34

to make sure that the light was put out. On his desk were spread a depressing number of accounts, bills, letters of reminder and his bank pass-book. He had evidently been compiling a list of his debts, for two sheets of paper were covered with columns of figures. Beside these rested a revolver.

Ismay experienced a most unpleasant shock on seeing this. Was it possible that Susan's absurd suggestion had any foundation in fact? He could not really have intended—— But her knowledge of her father served to calm her almost immediately.

It was not specially surprising to find that the revolver was unloaded. Also the columns of figures had been added up to an incorrect total. Putting both the revolver and the papers into the middle drawer of the desk, Ismay turned out the lamp and went upstairs to bed.

It was not until the next afternoon that Ismay had an opportunity to talk to Avril alone. When she had come up to bed after settling Father's problems for the moment, Avril was either asleep, or determinedly feigning sleep. But the next afternoon, while Ismay was doing whatever was humanly possible with Susan's maltreated tights, Avril came in from the garden with a big bunch of roses, which she proceeded to arrange in a bowl by the window.

'They look nice, don't they?' She stood back to regard them.

'Yes, they're lovely. Funny that our roses were always better than the ones at Estercourt, in spite of Great-aunt Georgina's three gardeners.'

'Um-hm. At least we're staying where the prize roses are.' Avril smiled reflectively.

Ismay glanced at her.

'Avril, I don't believe you're so terribly disappointed as the others, are you?'

'Perhaps not.' That gave away exactly nothing.

'Because you think you can get whatever you want in other ways?' Ismay's tone carried a direct challenge, because she knew how adroitly Avril could slide away from questions.

'Well, there *are* other ways, aren't there?'

Ismay's hands dropped into her lap.

'I don't know why we're fencing. Tell me, are you seriously thinking of that dreadful man's offer again?'

'He's not a dreadful man. Only a man who doesn't care a damn what other people think of him. And anyway, why is it more disgraceful to make the sort of bargain I am making than to live in the pockets of tradesmen who can't afford to have their bills unpaid but have to put up with it? At least my way is more honest. I'm giving value for money—or I suppose so.'

Ismay went rather pale.

'You *are* giving? What do you mean?'

Avril laughed with real amusement.

'I'm sorry, dear. That should still have been decorously in the future. You needn't be so agitated. It's none of it in the present—yet.'

'Then, for heaven's sake, forget this crazy scheme! I know it's awful that we owe so much. I know it's dishonest, just as you say. But we've got to alter that now. We always counted on that fortune coming one day. I see now—it's been the curse of our family. But we've got to have things on quite a different basis. You and I and Adrian must go to work—earn some decent income, and gradually pay off the debts. It's dull, I know, but it's the only honest way. *Your* suggestion——'

'My dear,' Avril interrupted coolly, 'have you any idea how much Father owes?'

Ismay was silent. For a moment she could see nothing but those pathetic, inaccurate calculations on Father's desk last night. When she looked up again she had still less colour in her cheeks.

'It's a ghastly amount, I know, but we must——'

'Listen, Ismay.' Avril was not heated about it, only quite determined. 'I'm twenty. I'm at the very beginning of my life—or at any rate, of the part of it that matters. I'm not going to start with the millstone of Father's debts round my neck. I'm sorry for him, poor darling, but it's been nothing but his own mismanagement that's landed him where he is. I don't doubt that Mother tried to push some sense into him years ago, and I don't doubt she was loftily talked down. Well, there's nothing to be done about it now. At any rate, there is nothing that *I'm* going to do about it. In the time-honoured phrase, I am going to live my own life.'

'You mean,' Ismay said deliberately, 'that you are going to become Keith Otterbury's mistress because you think it's "easy money".'

Avril bit her lip slightly and her colour rose a little.

'You're putting it as brutally as you can, aren't you?'

'Of course. How else should one put it? It's a pretty brutal fact.'

'It isn't so much the money, Ismay. Really, that isn't the attraction. It's being able to go away and study—to live somewhere where it's all colour and sunshine—not to have to crawl from day to day studying the petty details that matter so little but can spoil everything. I haven't got a beautiful nature. I'm not interested in Susan's tights and Father's moods and the price of new potatoes. I want to live carelessly and a little dangerously—to see the famous and beautiful things of the world before I'm too old to enjoy them. I'm sorry you're shocked and miserable about it—but that doesn't really alter it in the least.'

That part at least was true—Ismay could see it perfectly. There was no argument left that would appeal to Avril. She might as well stop the discussion now.

One could appeal to Father, of course. He would produce long and resounding speeches modelled on all the outraged stage fathers there had ever been. But what would be the good of that? Avril would withdraw into her own remoteness, and probably not even hear what he was saying. Then when the wind and thunder had died down, she would proceed exactly as she had intended.

Adrian?—No, Adrian had no more influence with her than Ismay herself. Less, probably, because he would grow impatient and sarcastic, or, alternatively, might take the point of view that if she insisted on making a fool of herself, it was really her own affair.

There was no one—no one at all to whom one could apply. No influence to balance against the influence of this practically unknown man to whom Avril seemed willing to consign her future life. It was ridiculous! There was so little on which the whole arrangement could have been based. With him it could hardly be more than a capricious whim—a matter of half-cynical amusement which *could* not be of great value to him one way or another.

Then might *he* be open to persuasion, to argument, to some sort of appeal to his sense of decency?

38

After all, there was nothing in all this to indicate how deeply the projected affair went with him. It was not too late——

Ismay looked thoughtfully after her sister as she turned and strolled out into the garden once more. And as she watched, resolution slowly hardened in her mind. A very disagreeable resolution—a frightening resolution, come to that—but one which was well worth taking. She would go and see Keith Otterbury herself, appeal to his better self, his common sense, his—well, whatever one did appeal to in a man of his sort.

Ismay felt better when she had come to this decision—but she felt worse when she came to put it into practical effect. It was all very well to think, 'I shall go and see Keith Otterbury. That's the solution.' But it made cold little shivers run over her when she had to think—'Shall it be this evening? Had I better leave it until tomorrow, or is it best to do it with as little delay as possible?'

It was Avril herself who decided her. She said something about staying in her room to write letters all the evening.

'I can't imagine anyone having enough letters to keep them going all the evening,' Susan said. 'And why not write them in the dining-room?'

'Because I don't want to have to help you with your Latin homework,' retorted Avril, who was gifted in these matters but indolent. 'Anyway, I really have heaps of letters to write. About six months' accumulation. I never think it's worth while doing them oftener, because you only get replies by return of post and have to start all over again.'

'Regularity in attending to one's correspondence is the

only sensible rule, my dear,' observed Father, who very seldom attended to his own correspondence, and never with any degree of regularity.

No one answered, so presumably they subscribed to the general principle without feeling that it had any uncomfortable application to themselves. Which was 'typical Laverhope,' as Adrian always said.

Ismay waited until their early supper was over. Then, taking her old blue coat from the peg in the hall, she went out of the side door into the garden, remarking casually to Adrian that she 'felt like a walk, but would not be long'.

For a moment she was afraid that Adrian would offer to accompany her. But he didn't. He evidently had affairs of his own to occupy him. That was one of the queer results of Great-aunt Georgina's will, thought Ismay. All the Laverhopes suddenly discovered that they had private concerns which must be worked out independently of the rest of the family. Avril retired to her bedroom, Father to his study, Adrian looked absently at her when she spoke to him, and now here was she herself going out on a sensational errand without the remotest intention of telling the others where she was going.

It was a warm September evening, and there was still a good deal of light lingering over the countryside. Immediately overhead the sky was soft and clear, but there were heavy clouds banked along the horizon, suggestive of a storm not so far off. Every now and then the trees moved agitatedly and without apparent reason, as though they knew the storm was coming, feared it a little, but knew there was nothing they could do but wait for it.

'I suppose that's rather how I feel,' thought Ismay.

She had pulled the coat over her shoulders, without

actually slipping her arms into the sleeves, but in spite of the warm evening, she shivered and drew the coat round her more closely.

By now, of course, she ought to have worked out something of what she intended to say to Keith Otterbury. That was, if she should find him in. For a moment her mind caught thankfully at the cowardly possibility that there might be a reprieve that way, but she brushed aside the thought again at once. No disagreeable task had ever grown easier for being put off. It would be bad luck, not good luck, if he should be out this one evening.

What *was* she going to say? What did one say to a man who proposed to conduct an affair with one's sister?

She found suddenly that she knew so desperately little about him. Nothing much more than the village gossip or the half-intrigued, half-spiteful remarks which his neighbours passed upon him. True, she had been introduced to him two years ago at the County Flower Show, but the introduction had been made by one of her father's less careful friends, and, before they had exchanged more than the barest conventionalities, Father had come up and removed her with skill and dignity.

At the ball last February, when he had danced with Avril, he had wanted her to dance with him too, but—a little to her relief, to tell the truth—she was able to say that her dances were all booked. Afterwards she caught him looking at her once or twice with those bold, smiling dark eyes of his, and she had thought uncomfortably at the time that he probably had not believed her. But he had not spoken to her again, and later, if ever she met him out riding, he simply greeted her as he passed and never made any attempt to speak to her further.

Now it was she who was to make the attempt—which was a horrid situation. Besides, she still had no idea what she was going to say.

The distance from the Laverhopes' house to Otterbury Hall was not more than half a mile in a straight line, but it took Ismay nearly twenty minutes of quick walking to reach it by way of the winding lanes. As she turned into the tree-bordered drive, the last of the evening light was fading, and overhead the stars were beginning to prick bright holes in a purple sky.

Otterbury Hall was not such an imposing place as its name implied. Starting as a large farmhouse more than a hundred years ago, it had been added to by successive owners in a haphazard and not very artistic fashion. The present owner's father, in the early days of his marriage, had made a real effort to bring the place into some sort of regular form and style. There had been a certain amount of rebuilding, which had succeeded in destroying the farmhouse character of the place but had fallen short of transforming it into a mansion.

Then his young wife had grown tired of the country. The hundred miles between Otterbury Hall and the London life she liked had become too much for her. On her insistence the place had been emptied except for a caretaker and his wife, and, for all practical purposes, Otterbury Hall had become uninhabited.

And so it had remained for considerably over twenty years, until Keith Otterbury had inherited the estate and had come there to live, something like five years ago.

The irregular bulk of the house rose before Ismay, black against the evening sky, flanked on either side by a great cedar tree. There was something faintly sinister about the place in this semi-darkness, and she felt that never in her life had she undertaken anything so disagreeable as the task that lay before her.

Her nervous tug at the great brass bell-pull must have had more strength in it than she knew, for it set the bell ringing quite violently in some remote region of the house. She could hear it in the silence which enveloped the rest of the house.

Then she heard footsteps crossing the hall, and a moment later the door was opened, to disclose a manservant who looked in some surprise at the slim girl who stood in the patch of warm, bright light from the panelled hall beyond.

'Mr. Otterbury—is he in, please?' Ismay spoke more hesitatingly than she had meant to, for a cool bold appearance would probably be her best line to take, and she had intended to make at any rate a calm entrance.

The man stood aside for her to enter.

'If you'll come in I'll inquire, madam. I think Mr. Otterbury came in a few moments ago, but I will make sure.'

Ismay came into the hall, and heard the front door shut behind her with a sensation bordering on panic.

'Will you come this way, please?'

She was ushered into a long, lofty room—again with panelled walls, but the concealed lights, which the man switched on as they came in, shed a warm, almost cosy glow around, and counteracted any impression of gloom.

Crossing to the window he drew great velvet curtains of a queer burnt-orange shade, and the dark, rather frightening night was shut out, and the world narrowed down to this pleasant, unalarming room.

Ismay gave him her name as 'Miss Laverhope' and then added rather hastily, 'Miss Ismay Laverhope'. To let Keith Otterbury imagine he was going to see Avril might lead to any amount of complications. Then she sat down in one of the deep, leather-covered armchairs, the man went out of the room, and she was left alone to the silence and her own thoughts.

Reassuring though the room might be, it could not make her forget the desperate nature of her errand, and Ismay felt that if she had to wait long, all her courage would disappear, and she would creep from the house again without having made a shadow of protest.

But she had not long to wait. Almost immediately she heard a curt voice say :

'Who did you say?—Good lord !'

A moment later the door opened again and the master of Otterbury Hall came into the room. He closed the door and stood there for a second or two—puzzled, amused, as though he hardly knew what to make of the situation. Then he came forward slowly, and as he did so Ismay rose to her feet—a little white, her eyes very dark blue with something like fear, her hair pale gold where the light caught it. Perhaps he liked the picture, because he narrowed his eyes very slightly, with admiration as well as puzzlement.

'Miss Laverhope'—he held out his hand—'what can I do for you?'

With a reluctance that was more obvious than she knew, Ismay put her hand into his, and at that moment he said casually :

'I don't bite, you know.'

She managed to smile then.

'Oh, I'm sorry. Did I look—scared?'

'A little. Won't you sit down again?'

Ismay sank back into her chair. But he stood where he was on the hearthrug, his feet slightly apart, looking down at her with that concentration of amused interest which she found terribly disconcerting.

He had evidently, as the servant had said, come in only a short while ago, for he was still in his riding-suit—which made him look even more overwhelming, thought Ismay, than he had at the County Ball. A tall and very powerful man, he seemed much too full of energy and suppressed movement for anything but the out-of-doors, and there was something almost flamboyant in his fine, dark colouring and the half-insolent way he carried himself.

On horseback all that seemed more natural. Here in this room there was something too alive and colourful about him, and Ismay found herself noticing in turn the way his thick, strong, black hair grew straight up from his forehead and then back, the way the dark eyes sparkled with half-cynical amusement, the unusually deep red of his firm, rather full lips.

'I suppose that's what one calls a sensual mouth,' thought Ismay, and then realised with a start that he was still waiting for her to speak.

'Mr. Otterbury'—her voice was soft and sounded nervous even to her own ears—'I expect you are very much surprised that I should come to see you like this, but——' She stopped.

'The pleasure outweighs the surprise,' he assured her with a smile. And then, 'Will you have a drink? It helps a lot when you're trying to say something difficult.'

'Thank you.' She supposed it might help.

45

He crossed the room and poured out something into a glass. When he gave it to her and she drank it, she realised it was brandy, and she wondered then if she had looked very much like fainting. Certainly the way he said, 'Better now?' sounded as though the idea had crossed his mind.

'Well then, let's start again.'

'It's about Avril,' Ismay stated, with a lack of finesse which horrified her, but apparently not him.

'Oh yes?' He gave no sign of intending to help her.

'Mr. Otterbury, I know it must seem that this is not my business, but I've come to ask you to give up this crazy idea that you and she have. I don't think you know Avril very well really—she's not at all—at all that sort of girl. She thinks it all sounds very romantic and exciting now. She's infatuated with the idea of life abroad and being able to paint and study and do what she likes, but she hasn't got a very clear sense of values and she doesn't know what she's giving up.'

Once she had started, Ismay found that the words came in a torrent, and even when she paused for a moment he made no attempt to interrupt her. Only waited for her to complete her statement.

'She doesn't even think that she's—she's in love with you——' that was out before she could stop it, though the quick upward jerk of his eyebrows made her falter a little. 'But I think she's probably been quite honest about that. Avril would be. When we thought for a few days that we were rich, she gave up this other idea entirely. She was *glad* to give it up. Then——'

'What made you think for a few days that you were rich?' he inquired, with interest, as though that were really important.

46

'Oh, didn't you know? I thought everyone in the district knew. Our great-aunt was supposed to have willed a fortune to my father—he's been waiting for it for something like fifty years. She died the other day, and when the will was read, she had left everything to charity.'

Keith Otterbury laughed then. Threw back his head and shouted with laughter.

'Good lord! The mean old trout.'

Ismay, who thought the expression offensive and the laughter even more so, glanced away nervously, wishing she were anywhere but in this room, and feeling that they were getting uncomfortably far away from the question of Avril.

He brought her back to it, however.

'So Avril intended to give me the slip when she thought the great-aunt's money would do instead? She has a fine business instinct, has Avril. But now she prefers gilded sin to honest poverty, is that it?'

Ismay opened her lips to assent to that, but closed them again without being able to produce the word.

'But the conscientious elder sister wants to save her from herself?' He looked even more amused.

'Mr. Otterbury, it isn't even as though it's a very serious matter to you. You——'

'What makes you think that?'

'Well, your whole attitude. Even now you're more than half laughing. You *can't* care very much for Avril, however lovely she is. She's unsophisticated, really. I know she sounds calculating over this matter——'

'She does indeed.'

'But it's an ingenuous sort of calculation. There's nothing experienced about her—no ground that you could

47

possibly have in common. After all, you're——'

'Yes?' He looked amusedly interested. She hesitated for a moment, and then rushed on in desperation.

'Very well then. You're blasé and hard-living. Everybody says so.'

'Do they indeed? Well, it's nice to have an insight into what other people are thinking, and this has certainly been an instructive talk. But there's one thing you've said which is undoubtedly true. I *don't* care for Avril, however lovely she is. There is only one girl in this district I care for, and that is you. Or rather—since we've agreed that I am blasé and hard-living—let us use the words appropriate to my character. You are the girl I really want. Not Avril.'

CHAPTER THREE

FOR several seconds Ismay assured herself that this was a bad joke. The sort of tasteless, ill-judged joke one might expect this man to make in the circumstances. But then she glanced at him and saw that those bright, insolent eyes were serious at last, and his hands were thrust deep into his pockets, pressed to his sides with a tension which had nothing jocular about it.

'I don't—know why—you should say such a thing to me just now,' she began. 'I haven't——'

'Because it's true,' he interrupted her curtly.

'It doesn't follow very well on your advances to my sister,' she retorted with some spirit, and she saw from his slight grimace that he acknowledged that as a hit. But he recovered his accustomed coolness almost immediately.

'Listen—we'll leave Avril out of this.' He sat down at last, in the chair opposite hers, and leant forward with his arms on his knees, his hands lightly clasped in front of him. 'I want you to tell me some more about this business of the family fortune. It's placed you all pretty awkwardly, I suppose, this caprice of the unlamented great-aunt?'

Ismay drew back slightly, and allowed her cool disgust to show in her face. The remark could hardly have been in worse taste, she thought, and her tone was cold and remote as she said :

'I don't think there is anything else to tell you about that. I hardly see that it's your business, in any case.'

He laughed slightly, unabashed by her snub, and made an impatient little gesture of almost literally putting aside her protest.

'No, of course it's hardly my business. Or at any rate, there's nothing to make it my business at the moment. But I don't want to leave it like that, you see. You've invited me to discuss one family problem—I find it has considerable bearing on another one. I think it's a trifle too late for you to put up your chilly little barriers and announce "no admittance here".'

She was silent for a moment. Then, because he really held all the cards, she yielded and said in the same cold little voice :

'What did you want to know then?'

'Just exactly how does this unfortunate will affect you all?'

'Well—very badly, of course.'

'You'd been counting on it very confidently?'

She hesitated.

'Are you speaking of me personally?'

'No, of course not.' He brushed that aside impatiently too. 'I don't think money means much to you—except in the way it affects the people you are fond of.'

Ismay considered that in silence, surprised to find how acute he had been about it. She had hardly thought of it herself, but now she knew he was right. Personally, she had not been bitterly hurt over the loss of the fortune. But she did most genuinely hate seeing the others so dreadfully disappointed.

'Very well then. I hate seeing the others so bewildered and shattered. Particularly my father. He had never had any reason to suppose the money would go anywhere else.

In fact, since he was a boy, she had told him that he would inherit it all. It was naturally a terrible blow.'

'Because he had traded on expectations, I suppose?—allowed himself a good many debts on the strength of them?'

'Mr. Otterbury, do you think you are adopting a particularly gentlemanly tone?' Ismay asked dryly.

'No,' he said, equally dryly. 'But then, you see, I am not a gentleman. I am what I believe is called "an outsider"—and, incidentally, I am extremely interested in getting to the bottom of this situation.'

'But why, exactly?'

'Partly because it concerns you.' He smiled straight at her in a bold, disconcerting fashion. 'Tell me—your father is pretty hopelessly in debt, isn't he?'

Ismay looked back at him with sad, angry eyes.

'I suppose it's common property in the neighbourhood. Yes, of course. He is up to his ears in debt. It isn't only *his* fault. It's the fault of all of us. We always arranged our lives on the assumption that we should be frightfully rich one day soon. It sounds awful, I know—like just waiting for someone to die in order to step into their shoes. But it had gone on for so long, you see. It started years and years before any of us were born—it was a family tradition. Great-aunt Georgina herself had insisted on it so often when my father was a boy, and she never hinted once that she had changed her mind. If we had been fond of her I don't expect we should have thought so much about it, because one *can't* think happily of inheriting from someone one loves. But she wasn't at all lovable. She never did a single thing that could endear her to anyone.'

'She wasn't fond of any of you?'

'Oh no. We always supposed that she had a sort of family feeling towards Father, but, so far as we were concerned, she preferred us to be afraid of her.'

'And were *you* afraid of her?' he inquired with interest.

'No,' Ismay said slowly. 'I don't think I was exactly. But I never went to see her with any sense of pleasure.'

'But you all kept up your spirits with the thought of the good time you would have when the money came along?' He sounded slightly sympathetic as well as amused that time.

'I suppose so. No one ever said as much, of course, but —yes, I'm sure Father thought of the lovely day when all the bills would be paid, and Adrian——'

'Your brother?'

'Yes. Adrian thought of being able to train as a doctor one day, and Avril'—she glanced at him nervously— 'Avril's great idea always was that she would go to Italy and study art and live a carefree existence.'

'And what did you want, Ismay?'

She felt startled and embarrassed at his casual use of her first name.

'I? Oh, I wanted them all to have what they liked, of course. And I thought it would be good fun to have the house done over so that it was all new and fresh. I'm afraid they were mostly material things that I thought about,' she confessed with a faint smile.

'But you thought of the general family content as well?'

'Yes.' The smile went. 'I did want them all to be happy and contented.' She sighed a little, because that was all so hopeless now. The best she could hope for was that this man would agree to leave Avril alone. And then she would have to go home and face a crop of insoluble problems—

have to know that every member of the family was unhappy and that there was absolutely nothing she could do about it.

He must have been able to read from her expression something of what she was thinking, because as she looked up again he said softly and a little mockingly :

'And it all depends on money.'

Ismay looked straight at him.

'Yes, I suppose it does. That sounds awful, doesn't it?'

'No,' he said coolly. 'Quite a lot of the most important things of this world depend on money. It is customary to pretend otherwise, but a truth is no less a truth because a certain number of people regard it as bad form.'

Ismay looked doubtful. She knew that Father, with all his preoccupation about debts, would, if pressed, have insisted in eloquent phrases that money had nothing whatever to do with things of the mind and spirit, and that these were really what mattered.

But then Father said a great many things that didn't make practical sense at all.

'Well,' Keith Otterbury said quietly, 'what are you going to do about it?'

Ismay looked at him in astonishment. Then a dash of indignant colour showed in her cheeks.

'I don't think it's for *you* to ask *me* that. I came to ask you to—to break off any connection with Avril. I should like to know what you mean to do about that. After your —your tasteless and callous remark about not caring for her, I suppose you won't still have the effrontery to force on the affair.'

She thought he would surely be insulted and angry at that, but he withstood her attack with imperturbable

53

calm. He didn't answer at once. Getting up from his chair, he thrust his hands into his pockets again and walked slowly the length of the room. Then, turning, he came back to where she was sitting and stood looking down at her with absolute gravity.

'You want me to promise to give up any connection at all with your sister?'

'Yes, that's it.' She was a trifle breathless, she found.

'And you'll take my word for it, if I say I promise?'

'Of course.'

'Not "of course" at all. But it's nice of you to put it that way,' he said ironically. 'Very well. I promise not to make any more advances to Avril or to put wicked ideas into her innocent head, on the single condition that you will marry me.'

For a second Ismay sat where she was. Then she jumped to her feet indignantly.

'Mr. Otterbury, will you please stop saying these ridiculous things! I—I don't deserve that you should make fun of me in this way, and indeed, *indeed* I have enough to worry me without your making stupid jokes about something that is very serious to me.'

'My dear, you couldn't be more serious than I am. Didn't you understand me when I said that it was you I wanted? I was perfectly serious then too. I do want you. I've admired and wanted you ever since I met you that day at the County Flower Show. But I'm not such a fool as to suppose one does anything but marry your kind. Until now there has never been the remotest chance of my being able to do any such thing. Now——'

'There is not the remotest chance now either,' Ismay told him flatly, and the haughty way she said that would

54

have delighted her father's heart. It seemed only to amuse
Keith Otterbury, however.

'Very well. I'll allow you the luxury of that retort.
Especially as you look so delightful when you are angry.
But don't you think you might consider first what I am
offering you before you refuse it so finally. I *am* asking you
to marry me, Ismay. That's not usually considered such an
insult to offer a woman. I am, as it happens, a very rich
man, and if you married me, you should have anything
you liked within reason—for yourself or, since it means so
much to you, for your family too.'

'Aren't you a little ashamed,' Ismay said quietly, 'to
think that first you tried to bribe one sister into being your
mistress and now, with a gracious raising of the price, you
try to bribe the other one into being your wife?'

He flushed darkly, and she saw he was very angry then.
But he kept his tone cool and steady as he answered her.

'You need not look at it like that at all. I very much
want you to say "yes" to me. I should be a fool if I didn't
tell you what advantages there were in marrying me. The
disadvantages are already patent to you, I suppose,' he
added with a short laugh. 'Don't reject the idea out of
hand, Ismay. Just think over whether you would like to
free your father from any more financial anxiety, enable
your brother to follow the career he wants, give Avril her
chance of going to Italy or wherever she wants without
paying a price for it, and ensure a good education for that
impudent little sister of yours—I forget her name—who
regards me, I believe, as a slightly picturesque criminal.'

For a moment Ismay made no attempt to answer that.
Partly because it was difficult to think of a snub sufficiently sharp to impress this man, partly because—useless

to deny it—the picture was a dazzling one. The idea that, at one stroke, one could make all the family happy once more had something almost intoxicating about it.

No debts for Father, no bitter frustration for Adrian, no dangerous temptation for Avril. The relief would be indescribable!

But of course the idea was fantastic. She looked up to find him regarding her with an attention that was not without a tinge of anxiety.

'I'm sorry, Mr. Otterbury. I don't know quite whether you mean all this generously or—or insultingly. But, in either case, I couldn't dream of agreeing, you know. The whole idea is rather—forgive me—rather silly.'

To her surprise, he smiled a little at that, as though in a sense he agreed with her.

'You mean it's too much like the melodramas of your father's youth?'

So he knew about that too!

'Well, yes, I do,' Ismay confessed.

'The villain of the piece proposes to buy the heroine by paying for her family's happiness?'

'S-something like that.' Ismay found she very much wanted to laugh, because she had suddenly remembered Adrian's absurd remark about 'Sir Jasper and the milk-maid'.

'Why are you smiling?' he wanted to know.

Ismay flushed quickly.

'Oh, I'm sorry. It was just—just that I thought of something rather silly.'

'Tell me.' He sounded peremptory but not annoyed.

'I think you might be angry.'

'No, I don't expect so.'

56

'Well, it's just that my brother always says that you—you're the kind of man who ought to be called "Sir Jasper" and be found—flirting with a milkmaid.'

'I believe "seducing the milkmaid" is the more usual and more telling expression,' he said gravely.

'I'm sorry. You must think me terribly silly. But when you said that about—about melodrama, I couldn't help thinking of what Adrian said. You mustn't mind. Families always have idiotic jokes and catchwords among themselves, you know.'

'I don't mind,' he told her, and added slowly, 'I suppose there *is* something rather silly and melodramatic about anyone who always acts on impulse.'

She was silent, wondering uncomfortably if he were at all hurt by the implication. But then one couldn't imagine that the Keith Otterburys of this world were particularly sensitive.

'So you absolutely refuse my—silly and melodramatic proposal?' he said at last.

'Mr. Otterbury, I'm sorry——'

'Miss Laverhope, you needn't be,' he retorted mockingly. 'The villain of the piece never suffers from wounded feelings, you know. All I ask is that you don't forget all about it.' She could hardly do that, Ismay thought. 'And if things become worse or unmanageable—or if you should for any other reason change your mind—please remember that my offer remains open, absolutely in the traditional manner.'

Ismay laughed a little in spite of herself.

'I think,' she said, with some relief, 'that you haven't been very serious about all this in any case.'

'Oh no, you're wrong there,' he assured her. 'If you

telephoned me tonight, saying you had altered your decision, believe me, I should go out and buy your engagement ring with the greatest pleasure tomorrow.'

That made Ismay feel uncomfortable again. It also reminded her that she was on the verge of leaving without having had a definite reply to her original request.

'About—Avril——' she began a trifle nervously.

'Oh yes. What about Avril?'

Ismay felt angry. If she had been the kind of girl to stamp her foot she would have stamped it then.

'I suppose I can take it that you will leave her alone?' She was tired now and there was a weight of anxiety still pressing on her, so that her soft voice sounded weary and impatient.

He seemed unaffected by that, however.

'My dear, I think you must allow to Avril and even to me the right which you reserve for yourself—that of deciding one's own life.'

'You mean you *won't* give me your word?'

'Don't you think this is all very much more Avril's business than yours?'

'But I've *told* you—she's young and silly and inexperienced. She doesn't know what she's undertaking. Don't you think you might be decent for once and see to it that she doesn't have the chance to make a fool of herself?'

'No. The "Sir Jasper" in me entirely revolts against such a noble impulse. What I think is that you had better go home and consider the offer I have made to you, and meanwhile I'll consider all that you have said,' he told her smilingly.

'You mean'—Ismay's voice was cold and horrified—'you mean you intend to put some sort of pressure on me

58

because of your influence over Avril?'

'I haven't said so. Come, it's certainly time you were home. It isn't specially good for your reputation to stay here much longer. Is this your coat?' He picked it up from the chair and held it for her.

There was nothing else to be done about it. She let him put her coat on for her, noticing subconsciously that he made not the slightest attempt to touch her—which seemed rather out of character.

'I'll take you back across the fields. It's much shorter that way.'

'Thank you. I don't need—or want—your company.' Ismay was surprised that she could be so flatly rude.

'Oh, you will be quite safe,' he assured her. 'And I shouldn't dream of letting you go home alone at this time of night. Come along.'

Ismay went, feeling slightly like a resentful child being taken out against its will.

There was no moon, but it was brilliant starlight. The threatening clouds had cleared away and the sky was one black velvet arch from horizon to horizon. Any other time she would have enjoyed the night, but walking across the fields with Keith Otterbury, she could only think, 'What a hateful man he is! I thought for a moment he was rather humorous and nice, but if he really won't help me about Avril, then he's just the sort of man everyone says he is.'

He allowed her the silence she seemed to prefer, only speaking once, when he was helping her over a stile which divided two of his fields.

'This,' he said gravely, 'is where I always arrange my interviews with the milkmaid.'

Ismay wished he had been a nice man, and then she

59

could have laughed at that. But, as it was, she permitted herself only the briefest smile, and perhaps by starlight even that was not apparent to him.

As she stepped down from the stile her hand was in his for a moment. There was a lot of support in that hand, she thought—it was warm, muscular, and exceedingly strong.

He took her right to the gate of her home and then gravely bade her goodnight. She thought she would pluck up courage to ask him just once more to reconsider his non-committal reply, but, on second thoughts, she desisted. Perhaps it was foolish to let a man like this see how terribly important the whole thing was. It merely told him how best to apply pressure to get what he wanted.

So she murmured a hasty goodnight, and ran round the house to the side door, where she could slip in without much likelihood of comment on the lateness of the hour.

But Ismay had reckoned without some unusual disturbance which had evidently taken place in her absence.

As she came in she was surprised to see that the light in the hall was blazing away, and almost immediately Avril came out of the dining-room. An agitated Avril—paler and showing much more sign of feeling than Ismay had often seen on her face.

'Oh, Ismay, there you are! Where on earth have you been?' But she didn't wait for a reply. 'Something so dreadful has happened. It's about Father——'

'*What* about Father?'

'Imagine! He tried to shoot himself. Yes, really. With his old service revolver.'

'Shoot himself?' Oh, why had she not taken him seriously last night? 'You don't mean he—did it—killed himself?'

'No, no, of course not.' Avril was unconscious of any humour in this oblique comment on the efficiency of Father's actions. 'He was only slightly hurt. But you can imagine the shock for us all. Adrian went at once and took the thing away before he could do any real damage. We sent for Dr. Marsh, and he's given Father a sedative and put him to bed. He assures us there is no serious injury, only of course it was a terrible shock for poor old Father himself.' Ismay noticed subconsciously that it was the first time any of them had ever called Father 'old'.

'Can I go to him?' Ismay had ripped off her coat, and spoke over her shoulder to Avril as she hung the coat on its peg once more.

'No, better not. He's probably asleep. Adrian stayed with him until he went to sleep. Dr. Marsh says there isn't any fear of his making—making another attempt. It was just a sudden impulse. I suppose he was in despair, Ismay, about the money situation. I don't know just how bad things are, but—— Oh, here's Adrian.'

Adrian, also a little pale but less obviously agitated than Avril, came down the stairs just then.

'Hello, Ismay. Where did you get to?' But he too did not wait for a reply. 'Avril's told you, of course? Come on into the dining-room. There's no need to stand in the hall while we discuss things.'

They went into the dining-room together. Unconsciously they grouped themselves round the table in this moment of family conclave, and as the light shone down on their young, fair, grave faces, there was something curiously alike in the three expressions. It was the first shadow of the necessity of facing responsibility alone.

It was Ismay who spoke first.

'Does Susan know?'

'No. She had gone to bed and, as usual, was sleeping like the dead.' For a moment they all felt Adrian had used an unfortunate simile. Then he added abruptly, 'I see no reason why she need know anything about it.'

'It *is* best that she doesn't know, I suppose?' Ismay hated mysteries, and knew Susan's talent for discovering them. The others were emphatic, however.

'Of course.' That was Avril, curt and much more practical than usual. 'She'd never be able to keep anything so sensational as an attempted suicide to herself. She'd probably think it was a distinction to have one in the family.'

Adrian smiled grimly.

'Well, I don't know about that. But certainly the fewer people who know, the better. That will help Father to get over it all the more quickly himself. If only it didn't cost so much to send him away somewhere—on a short cruise or something like that. But everything of the kind only adds more to the very cause that's worrying him. *Every-*thing costs so much money. Poor old chap, he must have been in a much lower state than any of us guessed.'

Adrian too called him 'poor old chap'—an expression no one would have dreamed of using to describe Father even a week ago. But then it was true—he did look old now. Ismay remembered she had thought just the same thing of him last night.

She looked up with a worried little frown.

'I feel I am rather to blame for letting this happen.'

'You, Ismay!' The other two looked astonished.

'Yes. I didn't tell you, but I found him last night in the study, reckoning up his debts, poor darling—I suppose for the first time in his life. The total must have given him an awful shock, particularly as it was wrong. And he had his revolver beside him on the desk. But it wasn't loaded, and I didn't think he even had any ammunition. I couldn't take it seriously. I just thought that it was one of his—his gestures, you know.'

The others nodded. They did know.

'I was a fool, though, not to remember that it wasn't a time when even Father would be trying to make an effect. I just comforted him a bit, and gave him hot milk and aspirin. He seemed so much better and quite cheerful when I left him. I would have taken the revolver and hidden it, only you know the terrible fuss he makes if we touch anything, and it—it would have looked as though *I* were getting silly ideas into my head, and it might have made him think seriously of something about which he was only play-acting.'

'Yes, I know what you mean,' Adrian said. 'But I wish you'd mentioned it.'

'I meant to.' Ismay was full of remorse. 'As a matter of fact, I meant to speak to *him* very tactfully about it myself, and persuade him to let me have the revolver, just to be on the safe side. But somehow—I know it sounds awful —I forgot. I—I was rather worried about something else. It's dreadful the way one means to do things, and—and doesn't,' she finished rather lamely.

She suddenly felt very much depressed. She always meant to do such a lot for the family—to look after them and see they came to no harm. And now she had done nothing about it when they were facing the greatest crisis of their lives. She had even let Father make this pathetically absurd attempt to end things, instead of finding some way—*some* way of helping him.

'If only there were something one could do to dig us all out of this ghastly hole!' Adrian exclaimed. 'I know it's mostly our own fault that we're in it, but that doesn't make the hole more attractive.'

'What you're asking for is a miracle,' Avril told him. She had got over the shock a little, and was returning more to her usual air of casual detachment. 'What is there, do you suppose, that could reinstate Father, make you a doctor and send me to Italy all in one wave of the wand?'

Adrian laughed slightly at that. But Ismay was absolutely still and silent. She was thinking how curious it was that Avril should have put it just like that. Put it as Keith Otterbury had when he had offered her the power to change the family fortunes. It was ridiculous, of course, that he had offered it—but the power was there, the offer was there, being kept open 'in the traditional manner', as he had laughingly told her. She got up suddenly, pushing back her chair sharply.

'I suppose,' she said, 'we might as well go to bed.'

The other two stood up.

'Yes. It's late enough.' Avril yawned.

'Ought someone to stay up with Father?' Ismay turned to Adrian again. 'What did Dr. Marsh say?'

'No, it's all right. He's had a sleeping draught. Dr. Marsh says he'll sleep until the morning now.'

'Isn't it queer,' Avril said as they locked up the house, 'being on our own like this? I mean without Father to tell everyone exactly what he thinks they ought to do next.'

'Yes,' said Ismay, and felt the weight of personal responsibility grow even heavier.

She went into the dining-room, where Adrian was alone, idly turning over the pages of a book, without paying any attention to what was printed there.

'What is it, Adrian?' She found that the slightest hint of preoccupation or worry on the part of any of the family was sufficient now to make her apprehensive. 'What's the matter?'

'The matter?' He looked up in surprise. 'Nothing.'

'Oh—I just wondered why you hadn't gone to bed.'

'I'm going.' He closed the book with a slam. 'At least—— Look here, Ismay, do you think we ought to have a look at those calculations of Father's and see just how deeply we *are* sunk? I don't want to turn over his private affairs, but this does concern the lot of us, and he is constitutionally incapable of telling us the real state of things—even if he were well enough to do so.'

Ismay bit her lip.

'Yes, I suppose you're right. There's no point in putting it off, and pretending to ourselves that things are better than they are. Coming now?'

Adrian nodded, and together they went into Father's study.

The light, when Ismay put on the lamp, shone on just as much confusion as there had been the previous night, and Adrian remarked grimly :

'You'd better take one pile of those bills and I'll take another. Perhaps we can work out something from them.'

Ismay sat down at the desk and began to turn over a depressing sheaf of papers. Adrian, standing at the side of the desk, did the same.

After a short silence Adrian said :

'Do you suppose Father ever paid *anything*?'

'Not if he could help it, I feel sure. Some of these date from—— Adrian, aren't there any receipts?'

'It doesn't look like it. Just a moment. These look more hopeful.' Adrian reached across Ismay and picked up half a dozen slips of paper. 'Yes, these are receipts for something. Something to do with the house——'

'The *house*!' Ismay put down the papers she had been holding. 'But there's nothing to pay on the house. It's ours. It belonged to Mother—don't you remember? It was the one thing that always comforted me—the thought that we had a roof over our heads. There wasn't even ground rent, Adrian. It's freehold. Oh, you must be mistaken. Let me see.' She leant over anxiously to examine the receipts in her turn.

There was a long silence. Then Adrian said:

'You see what it is, don't you?'

Ismay raised frightened eyes to his.

'A mortgage on the house? These are receipts for payments of interest?'

'Um-hm. The date on the last one is over a year ago too. That means he hasn't been keeping up the payments.'

'Then—then the house isn't ours at all?' Ismay said stupidly.

'That's what it looks like. I don't know the terms, of course. You can't tell from these receipts. But not paying interest on a mortgage usually leads to only one thing.'

'Adrian, *are we going to be without a home*?'

Her brother didn't answer.

'I know it sounds silly,' Ismay said at last, 'but I feel most awfully sick.'

'Oh, poor kid!' Adrian looked sympathetic. 'I know. It's a sort of panic. Sit quiet for a moment while I try to work things out. It mayn't be as bad as we think. Will you have something to drink, Ismay?'

'No, thanks. I've had one brandy already tonight,' Ismay said absently.

'Have you?' Adrian looked astounded. 'How did that happen?'

'Oh, I called in to see—to see Miss Peters,' Ismay explained hastily, choosing the name of the first acquaintance who came into her mind.

'Heavens! I didn't know she was a secret tippler.' Adrian grinned faintly as he bent over his calculations.

'Oh, she's *not*. Only I felt a bit faint and——'

Adrian glanced at her sharply.

'For heaven's sake don't you get ill, Ismay dear. That *would* be the last straw.'

'I'm not ill,' Ismay protested. 'Not the least bit. Don't go imagining things.'

'All right.' Adrian sounded absent again. And Ismay was silent, wondering a little why she didn't explain quite frankly what she had done that evening. She and Adrian had very few secrets between them, and he had really just as much right to know as she.

Or had he? Wasn't this perhaps entirely her own affair?

Suppose—just for the sake of argument—that she considered Keith Otterbury's offer. Then of course she could not tell any of them—least of all Adrian—the exact circumstances which led up to it. He would most certainly consider it a ridiculous and iniquitous idea. Well, it *was* ridiculous. Only not quite so ridiculous as it had seemed when it was first suggested.

Ismay was very tired indeed by now and, propping her elbow on the desk, she leant her head on her hand.

It must be wonderful to have heaps of money—enough money to have anything you wanted within reason.

Wasn't that the expression he had used? She wondered what Keith Otterbury considered 'within reason'. Something fantastically generous, she felt certain, because that somehow went with the character of the man. He did everything to excess.

Adrian looked up just then.

'I wish to God I knew some tame millionairess I could fascinate,' he said, with a sigh. 'It seems about the only thing that would cover all this disaster.'

'Is it *so* bad?'

'Are you going to be sick if I tell you how bad?'

'No.' She managed to smile faintly. 'I'd better know the truth. I can bear it.'

'Well, as far as I can see, the house has gone, Father owes a whack for Income Tax (I don't know how he contrives to do that, with next to no income), there are two or three dozen odd bills of varying amounts, and nothing to set against the lot except a handsome overdraft. I don't know whether he's been a fool enough to go to moneylenders, but there's a letter here that has got a nasty smell about it, to my way of thinking. It's obscure—but then moneylenders' letters always are, I understand. Anyway, there it is. Talk about the wolf howling at the door! It sems to have come in and made itself thoroughly at home.'

'Adrian, what on earth are we going to do?' Ismay's voice was very little more than a whisper.

'I don't know, my dear. We'd better go to bed now, for a start. It must be nearly two o'clock.'

She got up slowly and stiffly.

'We'll all three have to get jobs, just as soon as we can.' Ismay tried to make that sound hopeful, but she only succeeded in sounding very frightened.

'Jobs? Oh, I've got a job, as far as that's concerned.'

'You've got a *job*, Adrian! What sort of a job? How wonderful! Why didn't you tell me before?'

'It's not specially wonderful. Assistant and general run-about to old Astley, the chemist.'

'Oh, Adrian——' Ismay began. Then her courage really did fail, and a few tears gathered in spite of herself.

'I know. You're wondering just about how far what I earn will go among all that.' Adrian waved his hand in the direction of the papers on the desk. 'So am I.'

'No, it wasn't that.' Ismay shook her head. 'Anyway, I think it's wonderful of you to have gone out and got a job right away—*any* job. You are a good boy, Adrian.'

Her brother grinned a little and said again: 'Come on to bed.'

But all the way upstairs Ismay was thinking:

'And Keith Otterbury offered to see him through his medical training—and to give me anything else within reason.'

CHAPTER FOUR

LATE though it had been when she and Adrian went up to bed, Ismay lay awake, staring into the darkness, quite unable to drag her thoughts away from the problems confronting them all.

And then that fantastic scene at Otterbury Hall this evening! It was impossible not to go over that again and again, remembering a sarcastic inflection here, a hint of real generosity there, and wondering to what sum total all those impressions added up. Was it conceivable that one *could* take a man like that seriously?—that one could literally make oneself think, 'If I did marry him, this and this would happen? Could I put up with that? Or should I want to murder him after the first week?'

Ismay had never very seriously thought about marriage before. There had been dance partners and tennis partners and other social companions of her own age, of course. She had flirted a little—though never so much as Avril—and had even imagined herself in love once or twice. But none of it had ever gone very deep. For one thing, her family meant much more to her than anyone else, and, for another, few people in the neighbourhood had believed quite so implicitly in Great-aunt Georgina's fortune as the Laverhopes themselves had done. In consequence, she and Avril were generally thought of as 'pretty as a picture and twice as charming—but without a penny to bless themselves with'. The mothers of eligible sons, therefore, preferred not to have them taken *too* seriously.

None of this had ever seemed to matter before—she had enough of the casual, carefree Laverhope temperament for that—and she had been willing to put everything off until a golden future should change the situation for them all, leaving her rather freer to live her own life in some vague pleasant way she had never quite mapped out.

Now all that was changed. They were facing stark realities—urgent and bitter decisions. And in this new, harsh world, Keith Otterbury's offer had a certain crude value which transformed it from an insulting absurdity to something which must be weighed and considered.

'It isn't as though he didn't mean it,' thought Ismay. 'It was a preposterous offer, but it was genuine. For some reason he really does want me to accept.'

And then she wondered why it was marriage he had offered her instead of what was usually delicately referred to as 'the other thing'. He had said something about knowing that one didn't offer 'her kind' anything else. But then it seemed he had offered that to Avril without any particular qualms. And Avril had accepted. That might, of course, mark the difference between Avril and 'her kind'.

'Perhaps that was what he meant,' Ismay reflected. 'Anyway, it's true, of course. I wouldn't have taken on that in any circumstances. But marriage is different—at least, I suppose it is. Anything would seem rather like an affair with that kind of man, though.'

Still, that was hardly the point. If *she* accepted what he offered, she could save the whole family from disaster without doing anything that could shock even her father's most delicate sensibilities. If Avril accepted, it simply

71

meant that she would ruin her own life, do nothing whatever to help the others, and shatter Father still more, because he would take anything like that very, very hardly. It was not only that he would play the rôle of outraged parent to perfection—he would *feel* the outraged parent. Father lived his rôles with almost pathetic intensity.

'And Avril will accept, of course—unless I do first,' thought Ismay with a realism which was not untinged with grim amusement. 'And that, I believe, would be even worse than the mess we are in at the moment.'

She listened, as she had so often before, to Avril's quiet, untroubled breathing. She slept like a child. She always did. But then Avril *was* rather like a child. A precocious, determined and very charming child. How *could* one argue a realistic problem with someone whose sense of values had practically no relation to the realities of a grown-up world?

'I can't let her do it,' thought Ismay. 'I could beat her for being such a criminal little idiot—but I can't let her do it. It's too dreadful a way to learn one's lesson.'

Then if Avril was not to be allowed to spoil her life there was only one way to stop her. One didn't want to think of it in detail, but——

As Ismay fell asleep in the first faint light of the dawn she remembered what Keith Otterbury had said to her— 'If you telephoned me tonight, saying you had altered your decision, believe me, I should go out and buy your engagement ring with the greatest pleasure.'

'There isn't time tonight,' thought Ismay, and then her eyes closed.

The next morning Susan's inquiries about her father

were many and detailed, so that Ismay began to wonder, with an irritation born of her short night, whether she possessed some perverse intuition which always told her the right—or rather, the wrong—time to ask questions.

'How funny that he should be ill just now! He's not sort of pining, is he?—I mean, about the money?'

'No, I don't think so.'

'It's a most 'straordinary thing!'

'Why?' Adrian wanted to know. 'People are ill sometimes.'

'Oh yes. But for *reasons*. Like a cold, or being sick, or having an accident.'

They all felt she was getting uncomfortably 'warm', and Ismay said hastily:

'He's just run down, I expect. And of course it must have been a great shock to find he was—well, that Great-aunt Georgina had done what she did.' Then to change the subject she added firmly, 'But isn't it splendid?—Adrian has got a job already.'

It was not, however, a very happy diversion.

'A job? *Adrian?*' Adrian's youngest sister looked incredulous. 'But whoever would want to pay him to do anything?'

'Thanks. Don't mind my feelings.'

'But it's true.' Susan was unmoved. 'What sort of a job?'

'Assistant to old Astley,' Adrian told her curtly.

'Do you mean an *errand* boy? Or do you mean swot in his time and he'll pay you for it? I call that——'

'Susan dear, you'll be terribly late for school,' Ismay interrupted, and fortunately this was nothing less than the truth.

There followed the usual frantic search for books which

had been mysteriously mislaid, punctuated by pathetic wails about the lateness of the hour. The miniature storm culminated in Susan erupting from the front door and rushing to the gate, declaring that never, never had anyone been so late as this before, and it would be much better to stay at home and say she had a headache.

Adrian looked after her out of the dining-room window.

'Did we all make the same unspeakable hullabaloo at that age?' he asked with genuine interest.

Ismay laughed.

'I can't imagine that Avril did, and I don't think boys care about being late or forgetting books so much as girls do.'

'I don't think Susan *cares* exactly,' Adrian said, smiling too. 'It's hard to imagine her caring about anything. It's a lucky temperament to have.'

Ismay wondered if there were anything she could say to him which would soften the harshness of the present situation as outlined by Susan. But, on the whole, she decided, it was better to say nothing. Rather too much had already been said. She contented herself with saying :

'When do you start this job, Adrian?'

And when he said shortly, 'Next Monday,' she thought with genuine relief :

'Well, I ought to be able to settle things long before then. I wish I could tell him now that he won't have to do it for long.'

Instead, she went upstairs to see her father—to receive his half-ashamed, half-airy explanations of what had happened.

'A most unfortunate and absurd accident,' he told her rather feebly, but watching her with a transparent anxiety

74

which showed how eager he was that the real truth should not be known.

'Yes,' Ismay agreed soothingly. 'It only shows how careful one ought to be with firearms.'

'I had no idea that it was loaded, of course.'

Ismay thought of the unloaded revolver which had been on the desk two nights ago.

'Of course not,' she said gently, and heard him give a sigh of relief. 'We must all be thankful it wasn't more serious. Adrian gave the revolver to Dr. Marsh. He will take it to London with him next time he goes, and sell it. It isn't a thing we're likely to need, and it's best out of the way.'

'I dare say you're right.' Father looked half uneasy and half relieved. Ismay thought he was probably glad to have temptation out of the way, but was wondering what on earth the alternative was. It was nice to feel one was not dead, but something of a problem to find one was alive.

'I shouldn't worry about anything if I were you.' It was funny how she had fallen into the way of speaking to Father as though he were about Susan's age. 'You just have plenty of rest, and don't think about anything but getting well. Things are going to be much better than you ever expected.'

'Are they?' He looked at her in an expectant way she had never seen before. Rather as though he had lost the one solution he himself had once had for all difficulties, and now he must look to someone else to supply all the answers.

'Oh yes.' Ismay smiled at him, her mind completely made up.

But she was glad, all the same, that he accepted the generalisation without asking for further details. However firm she might feel about the essential decision, she was not in a mood to discuss it.

Seeing that Father was inclined to go to sleep, she went quietly from the room.

For an hour or two at any rate, her time was her own. There would be no better opportunity than this, and delay was not only useless—it was dangerous. There was no telling what decision Avril might already have taken. At the moment she was harmlessly engaged in sketching an old tree in the garden. And, without a word to her, Ismay slipped out of the side gate, unhailed and unobserved.

At first she walked quickly, intent on her errand. Then she realised how hot it was and that even under the trees there was very little relief from the blazing sun. The sky was a deep, almost sapphire blue, softened only by a heat haze, and the very faint breeze which stirred the leaves from time to time scarcely seemed to reach farther than the extreme tree-tops.

Even her yellow linen frock, with its short sleeves and its white collar turned far back from her throat, seemed heavy and oppressive, and she could feel the heavy waves of fair hair clinging damply to her forehead.

Well, her errand ought to be enough to send cold shivers down her back, she reflected grimly. And then she stopped and listened intently, because, away in the distance, she had detected the sound of horse's hoofs.

It would not necessarily be Keith Otterbury, of course. A good many people in the district still preferred horses to cars. But whoever was coming was riding fast, and he almost invariably did.

Even before he turned the last bend in the lane, she knew it was he. He, on his part, recognised her at once, and reined in his horse. He didn't say anything for the first moment—just sat there smiling down at her, amused, quizzical and just a trifle insolent.

'Good morning, Mr. Otterbury,' she said at last.

'Good morning, Miss Laverhope,' he retorted a little mockingly. 'What a coincidence that I should meet you today of all days.'

'No, it's not a coincidence. I was coming over to your place. I wanted to see you.'

'You *wanted* to see me?' He swung off his horse, slipped the reins over one arm, and came slowly up to her. 'I'm flattered.'

'Well—"wanted" is perhaps not quite the word.' She couldn't resist that. 'I—I had to speak to you.'

'On business?' He was studiedly polite.

'I suppose one might call it business.' Her eyes fell, for the first time. 'It—it was about what we discussed last night.'

'I don't think one could call that business at all.' She knew from his tone that he was smiling. 'I should certainly call that pleasure.'

Ismay thought she would have called it something else, but she abandoned that part of the discussion.

'Anyway, I had to speak to you. Because—I did what you suggested—thought over very carefully what you had said. And I remembered you said that if—if for any reason I changed my mind——' she stopped.

He had made not the slightest attempt to interrupt her, and now he made no attempt to help her out. After a long pause, she said baldly :

77

'Well, I've changed my mind. That's what I was coming to tell you.'

'And what made you change your mind, Ismay?' He spoke quietly, almost sombrely for him.

'Does that matter?'

'No. But it's interesting.' He reverted immediately to his careless manner when she shot that resentful glance at him.

'Well—something happened last night which made me realise how hopelessly involved we are. There seems absolutely no way out unless one of us makes a rich marriage. I'm prepared to make it,' she finished grimly.

He laughed softly at that, much more amused than annoyed by her deadly candour.

'So you propose to marry me simply and solely for my money?'

'No.' Ismay raised angry eyes and looked straight at him. 'I don't think that would be sufficient in itself. But there's the question of Avril too. I can't let her smash up her life like that.'

'You prefer to smash up your own life?'

'That's—different. Besides, marriage is different from—that.'

'In all essentials it is the same,' he told her, and that bold, careless glance of his did nothing to soften that. 'But I admire your self-sacrifice and your—candour.'

'There isn't much point in pretending, is there?'

'No, Ismay. I think perhaps that's what I—like so much about you. I don't believe you pretend about things, even to yourself. You certainly haven't put up any pretence to me about this marriage of ours.'

She was silent, slowly digesting the phrase, 'this marriage of ours'. Then she looked up again at last, her blue eyes very dark and a little weary because of her sleepless night.

'Is it—settled, then?'

He nodded, his eyes still on her.

'It's settled, Ismay.'

'You promise to leave Avril alone?'

'I do.' He smiled at her earnestness.

'And you really will—will——'

'Finance all the family dreams? Oh yes. You'll have to tell me in detail what it is they want and we will arrange it.'

'Very well. Thank you.' That came reluctantly. 'And when—when do you want to marry me?'

He laughed aloud at that.

'I want to marry you right away—tomorrow, today, if it were possible. I've waited long enough for you. Two years! But I suppose you want a little more time than that. At the moment I think you've hardly reached the stage of knowing that you are engaged to me, and that it's therefore your duty and privilege to kiss me.'

His eyes were sparkling with amusement, but Ismay looked at him in something like horror.

'I don't want to kiss you.'

'But you'll have to come to it eventually, you know.'

'Do you mean that I must—I must pretend to be fond of you?'

'We—ell'—she wondered how he could possibly laugh at this moment, 'we won't set too high a standard. But I think you must contrive to appear mildly devoted in public.'

'We're not in public now,' she reminded him coldly.

'Meaning that you have no intention of kissing me at this moment?'

Before Ismay could reply, their conversation was suddenly interrupted by a tremendous clap of thunder, and without the slightest warning the rain came lashing down through the trees, as though determined to pierce any scrap of shelter there might be.

'Oh!'—Ismay shrank slightly before the ribbon of lightning that seemed to thread its way through the sky. It showed up the banks of heavy cloud which had miraculously gathered, unnoticed, in the last ten minutes. Then the thunder crashed again, and at the same moment there was the rending sound of splitting wood.

'Here, we must get out of this!' He caught her by the arm, using his other hand to quiet his frightened horse. 'Can you ride?'

'No, I'll stay here. It will pass.'

'No, you won't. There's no protection from the rain, and there's danger from the trees. I can manage you.'

'On that horse?'

'Of course.' He mounted as he spoke and then leant down to her. 'Give me your hand.'

'No! I can't ride and I——'

'Don't be a little fool. Give me your hand—so. Now put your foot on mine.' Half stunned by the thunder and the rain, she did as she was told, and he swung her up in front of him more easily than she would have thought possible.

The horse was more nervous now, and it seemed to Ismay that the great black head dipped away in front of her, leaving her no security. Instinctively she clutched hold of Keith Otterbury.

'You're all right.' He laughed down at her. 'I'll have

you home in three minutes.'

But 'home' in this case appeared to be his own place, and he was cutting across the fields now, away from the road. Ismay glanced in something like terror over her shoulder.

'You're not going to leap that gate?'

'Of course.'

'Oh, I *can't*——'

'Be quiet. You haven't got to do anything. Shut your eyes if you don't like it.'

She shut her eyes, but that hardly seemed enough, and as she felt them leave the ground, she hid her face against him. Afterwards she was angry with herself and a good deal ashamed, because it all seemed fairly easy, the way Keith did it. But he laughed a good deal at her fear, and held her close against him in a way which made her very much aware of the hard muscle of his left arm.

'There, you're all right. We're home now.' He lifted her down. 'Run in out of the rain. I'll take Jade round to the stables.'

Someone must have heard or seen their arrival (Ismay hoped it was heard), for as she stepped into the porch, the door was opened for her by the servant who had admitted her last night. This time his face expressed no surprise, and he took her at once into the room where she had been before.

'Did you get very wet, Miss Laverhope?' He even seemed concerned about her.

'No, thank you.' She supposed they must have been riding before the storm, because Keith's figure seemed to have saved her from the worst of the rain. 'It's nothing much. I'm afraid Mr. Otterbury got most of it.'

He came in just then, taking off his wet riding-coat as he came. (Father would have died rather than do such a thing in the presence of a lady, Ismay remembered subconsciously, but she noticed also what a fine figure Keith was in shirt sleeves.)

'Are you all right?' He glanced at her critically.

'Oh yes, thank you.'

'You'd better get us some coffee, Palmer.'

'Yes, sir.'

She thought he would be almost certain to tease her when Palmer had gone, laugh at her for having been frightened, and declare that he must make a better horsewoman of her than that—or something equally offensive. But he didn't. Instead, he looked at her serious face and asked :

'Are you angry, Ismay?'

'Oh—no.' Ismay smiled very slightly then. 'I was just thinking that I made rather an exhibition of myself just now. I thought you might be the one to be angry—or at any rate scornful.'

He looked surprised. But all he said was :

'It takes a great deal more than that to make me angry.'

'Or scornful?' inquired Ismay, to whom that was nearly as bad as anger.

He grinned at her then.

'Could *I* presume to be scornful of one of the lovely Laverhopes? I simply shouldn't dare, my dear.'

She gave a vexed little laugh and turned away to look out of the window.

'My brother—Adrian, you know—simply loathes that description of us. He says it's our curse to look decorative in any circumstances, and he almost wishes he had a squint.'

'He may wish any misfortune he likes to his own eyes,' retorted Keith Otterbury coolly, 'but he mustn't dare to wish to change your beautiful eyes in the least.'

He was standing close behind her when he said that, but although she was acutely conscious of him, she refused to turn round.

'Ismay, when the storm broke, we were interrupted in a most interesting conversation.'

'Were we?'

'You know we were.'

She looked steadily out of the window.

'Haven't you anything to say to me?'

'Nothing—except that I think it's stopped raining now and it's time I went home.'

'You little devil !' he laughed softly, 'are you presuming on my assertion that it takes a lot to anger me?'

She turned then and looked up at him.

'Are you angry with me?'

For some reason his eyes widened as though he were slightly startled. He put his arms round her, but very lightly, so that they just encircled her but hardly touched her.

'No, Ismay, I'm not angry with you. But why don't you kiss me?'

She looked away from him.

'I will, if you insist.'

'You know I'm not going to insist, don't you? I may have my faults, but I've never yet kissed a woman against her will.' ·

It was in Ismay's mind to ask him how many he had kissed with their consent. But it was a moment for sharp repartee, and she said instead :

'It's enough for today to know that I'm engaged to you. I don't—want to kiss you. I'll kiss you some other time when I'm more used to it all.'

'Hm-hm.' His eyes were suddenly flickering with amusement again. 'In the true Laverhope tradition. You'll pay me tomorrow, eh?—but never today.'

'You—beast !' Ismay said. And, very much more to her surprise than his, she raised her hand and struck him smartly across the cheek.

At this most interesting moment, Palmer chose to return with the coffee.

He must have been a very well-trained servant indeed, Ismay decided afterwards, because he certainly contrived to give the impression that he had heard and seen nothing at all. Even when his master turned towards him, rubbing his cheek with a reflective smile, Palmer simply said :

'The coffee, sir.'

'Oh yes, Palmer—the coffee. Thanks.'

He came over to the coffee-table and began to pour it out.

'White or black, Ismay?'

'Oh—either. White, please.'

'Sugar?'

'Yes, please.'

'How many?'

'One, please.'

'Here you are.' He brought it over to her. 'Now I know exactly how you like your coffee.'

She raised her eyes reluctantly to his face.

'I'm sorry,' she said.

'Are you? All right. So am I.'

It was impossible to tell from his expression just how he meant that, and for a minute she wondered if he were simply sorry she had struck him, because of the repercussions that must follow.

'Does it make you feel—differently?'

'About what, Ismay?'

'About marrying me.'

'No. Was it intended to?'

'Oh no. Only I thought——'

He laughed.

'You don't suppose a man sets his heart on something for two years, and then lets himself be put off because of a rather well-deserved slap in the face, do you?'

Ismay didn't answer that. She was wondering what his heart had to do with it.

'Well, I think the rain has really stopped now, and if you're determined to go home, now is the moment to choose. May I take you?'

'No, please not. You see, I'd rather——'

'Prepare them for the shock?'

'Well, at least there is a great deal to explain, and one simply couldn't do it at lunch-time, with Susan coming in from school.'

'What has Susan to do with it?'

'Oh, quite a lot. You don't know Susan yet. She always wants to know the why and wherefore of everything.'

'H'm. That's going to be a bit difficult in this particular case, isn't it?'

'Yes. That's why I don't want you to come just now.'

'Very well. But do I come later and ask your father's

permission to marry you—or what is the family procedure?'

'Father would like that awfully, of course,' Ismay said seriously. 'But he's not quite well just now.'

'Is he ill?'

'Well—it was just a slight accident.' She had an uncomfortable impression that he could see right into her mind and knew just exactly what had happened. 'I think —I think I'd better telephone and let you know when it would be a good time to come.' She couldn't imagine there would ever be a 'good' time for introducing her astonished family to this unexpected fiancé.

'Very well.' He seemed willing to let her have it her own way. 'Don't keep me waiting too long, that's all.'

'No,' Ismay promised. 'I'll ring you this evening, I expect.'

He let her go then, telling her, with a final touch of mockery, that she could go home through the fields as they were 'practically her fields now'.

Ismay hurried as soon as she was out of sight of the house, for it was late already, and if she were not in time for lunch there would be some sort of comment.

But she was unlucky. Even as she came in, Susan leapt to her feet with the agility of a jack-in-the-box and exclaimed :

'Ismay Laverhope, what on *earth* were you doing, dashing around the countryside on Mr. Otterbury's horse, and he with his arm round you?'

'*What's* that?' Adrian looked up from the newspaper. 'Is that why you've been hopping mad ever since you came in? Not that it's your business, of course,' he added, a little too late.

86

'It *is* my business. It's everybody's business, I should think,' Susan protested. 'I couldn't *believe* my eyes. Carol Elthorpe and I were coming home from dancing, and we'd taken shelter under that big oak at the end of Quentin Lane——'

'Never shelter under trees in a thunderstorm,' her brother interrupted, in an effort to save Ismay from further questioning. 'It's a most dangerous thing to do.'

'Well, *we* hadn't got anyone to dash up on horseback and whisk us off to shelter like a Wild West film. And the rain was coming down fit to drown anyone. And then we saw Mr Otterbury dashing across the fields on that big black horse of his and there was someone with him, and I said to Carol, "You'd think he'd been abducting someone, wouldn't you?" And she said, "My goodness, it's your sister, Ismay." And I *very* nearly fainted,' concluded Susan who looked in blooming health.

'I'm sorry it all looked so hair-raising, Susan.' Ismay made that as cool as possible. 'But it was simply as you thought yourself—that we were getting in out of the rain as quickly as possible.'

'Yes, I *know*. But how did it come to be Mr. Otterbury who rescued you?'

'It wasn't a "rescue", Susan. We just happened to be talking and—well, when it rained, he kindly took me on his horse to shelter, that's all.' She wished fervently that Susan would indeed accept that as 'all'.

'But I can't understand how *you* were talking with him,' Susan insisted. 'Now if it had been *Avril*——' She stopped as Avril came into the room.

'If what had been Avril?' inquired her sister, with only the faintest interest.

'Oh, nothing,' Susan said hastily, with an amount of heavy discretion that would have made the least suspicious person begin to wonder.

Avril looked round slowly, and oblivious of the fact that their daily help had just brought in the lunch and was setting it on the table, she asked :

'Why, what is the mystery?'

'It isn't a *mystery*, exactly,' Susan said. 'It's just rather 'straordinary. Ismay was talking with Mr. Otterbury when the storm came on, and he took her on his horse, and just dashed off home with her—like a highwayman.'

'He didn't behave in the least like a highwayman,' Ismay exclaimed with considerable irritation.

'*Ismay* was with Keith Otterbury?' Avril repeated slowly. 'But I didn't know you even knew him.'

'Well, I do.' Ismay sat down and began rather deliberately, to serve out lunch.

'Funny—I didn't know you did, either,' Adrian said. 'I shouldn't have thought he was your kind exactly, Ismay.'

'Wouldn't you? I like him very much, as a matter of fact.'

'*Like* him? What an odd thing to say.' Adrian gave her a puzzled look. 'At least, I mean what an odd thing to say of a man like Otterbury. He's rather——'

Ismay set down her knife and fork with a little clatter.

'Don't say any more, Adrian, because—because—— Well, I didn't mean to tell you all quite like this, but—I'm going to marry Keith Otterbury. We got engaged this morning.'

'Marry !'

'Engaged !'

Adrian and Avril spoke simultaneously, while Susan for once could produce nothing but a sort of crow of sheer astonishment and excitement.

'Yes, I know it must seem frightfully sudden and inexplicable. But—but I've really known him, on and off, for quite a long time. It isn't really so sudden as—as it seems,' she finished lamely.

Adrian said nothing at all for a moment. Then looking straight at Ismay, he said :

'I don't think we're in quite such a tight corner as all that, Ismay.'

'I don't know what you mean.' Ismay's tone was perfectly steady, though she dared not look at Avril, or, to tell the truth, at Adrian.

'Oh yes, you do.'

'Well, *what* do you mean, Adrian?' Susan wanted to know. But no one took any notice of her.

'If you think I'm marrying Keith because we're in a tight corner and he's rich, you're quite mistaken,' Ismay told the lie with surprising earnestness.

'Are you going to tell me, Ismay, that you're in love with him?' Adrian asked quietly.

Ismay saw then that it was all or none.

'Yes,' she said, without hesitation.

Avril gave a very slight laugh, while Susan sucked in her breath and remarked :

'Fancy that now ! Well, they always *say* it's sudden.'

Adrian went on with his lunch in silence, and Ismay stole a glance at Avril. It was hard to tell from her expression what she was thinking, but Ismay somehow gathered that this extraordinary announcement was a relief rather than a disappointment to her.

And she might well be relieved, of course! She probably guessed that she would get most of what she wanted from her sister now, and there would be nothing to pay in return. Not even 'tomorrow'.

'I *never* heard of anything so 'straordinary!' For once Susan's babbling was something of a blessing. 'I think it's really rather romantic myself. And of course it's frightfully convenient that he's so rich. It doesn't seem to matter about Great-aunt Georgina now.'

Adrian gave her a withering look at that, but Ismay rather wanted to hug her. It was all very crudely expressed, but it was nice to hear *someone* put it into words. It didn't matter so much about Great-aunt Georgina now.

CHAPTER FIVE

It was fairly late in the afternoon when Ismay sought out Avril, for although she felt she *must* have some sort of a talk with her sister, Ismay found that Avril was not specially anxious, on her part, to say very much.

Ismay found her at last—out in the garden, sketching once more. An old mackintosh cape was spread on the still damp grass, and Avril sat there with a sketching-block on her knees, apparently oblivious to everything else.

Ismay came and sat down on a corner of the mackintosh, watching Avril in silence for a few minutes.

Avril looked up once and said, 'Hello', and then went back to her work. After a while Ismay went straight to the point.

'Avril, are you—angry with me?'

'No.' That sounded genuine enough. 'Why should I be angry?'

'I thought you might feel—sore about my—my engagement to Keith. I didn't mean to tell you just like that at lunch-time, you know. I meant to do it much more tactfully.'

'Yes, I'm sure you did.'

'Avril, please do tell me. It wasn't a case of your feelings being involved, was it? You weren't—fond of him, after all?'

'No,' Avril said. 'Nor are you either, are you?'

Ismay shrugged. It was useless to pretend with Avril, who already knew so much of the situation.

'No. But I'm not telling anyone else that.'

'I won't tell either,' Avril said, as though she thought Ismay might like that reassurance. 'Is it some weird idea of saving me from taking the downward path?'

'No.' Ismay didn't like to hear it described like that. 'It's just—everything. I'd better tell you, I think. You have some sort of right to know. I'm afraid you'll be wild, Avril, but I went to him yesterday evening, and told him I knew about you two——'

'You—*what*?' Avril raised her head and stared at her sister.

'Yes, I know it must seem awful to you, but to me it seemed the only thing to do. I *couldn't* let you ruin your life, Avril—for it would have been that. And at the same time I couldn't get you to listen to argument. There was nothing left but to go to him, and ask if I could make him do the decent thing.'

'And what did he say?' Avril asked curiously. She seemed singularly free from anger—only very much interested to hear what had happened.

'That it was not my business, of course. Which I suppose was true, in a way. I think he knew quite well that there was no—affection about it, Avril. With you, I mean. But anyway, I can't imagine you would have been anything but honest about that.'

Avril nodded, presumably in agreement with this.

'I finally asked him outright to—to give you up, to let the whole dreadful idea finish before it had begun.'

'And then what did he say?' Avril never took her eyes from her sister's face.

'He said—he said he would do so if I would marry him—and that he had always wanted to marry me, anyway.'

'He said that?'

'Yes.'

'And nothing else at all?'

'Well, nothing material.'

'How extraordinary,' murmured Avril, and went on sketching. 'But you didn't accept there and then, Ismay, surely? You said just now that it wasn't only because of me.'

'No, of course not. I turned the idea down pretty flat. I think I was very rude about it. But he didn't seem to mind. Only he told me that the offer remained open and that I was to think over all the things he could do for us all if I would let him. He was willing to pay Father's debts and pay for Adrian's training—and—and you can go to Italy, after all, Avril. He's willing to finance that too.'

'Is that true?' Avril said slowly.

'Oh yes.'

'And all this because you're marrying him? Ismay, he must be terribly—keen on you.'

'I don't know. I think perhaps it's just the idea of being able to have something—someone—he never expected to get.'

'Maybe. He is that sort of man, of course.' Avril spoke coolly, as though she had had very little to do with him, but could catalogue him quite easily. Then after a moment she asked, 'Are you very—miserable about it, Ismay? I can see you aren't exactly happy, of course.'

Ismay was silent, considering that.

'No, I don't think "miserable" is the word. I'm so frantically relieved, for one thing, that it will get us all out of the terrible hole we were in. It was much worse even than you knew, Avril. Even the house had gone—mortgaged, and the interest not paid up. I simply don't know where we should have turned if this hadn't happened. And then I couldn't bear to think of Adrian dragging out his youth and enthusiasm in a dull job. He's clever and he wants to work in a big way. He could do it too, if he had the chance. As it was, we hadn't even the money to pay his fare to London. I can't pretend it isn't heavenly to have all that settled after all.'

'Um-hm.' Avril looked reflective. 'I suppose it would be tactless to ask what you really think of Keith?'

'No,' Ismay said. 'But it would be useless. Because I don't even know myself. How can I? I hadn't exchanged more than half a dozen words with him before this happened.'

'It doesn't sound a bit like you, Ismay.' Avril seemed very intent on what she was doing.

'It *isn't* a bit like me. But what can we do? We've been pitchforked into the world of reality and told to sink or swim.'

'And we looked remarkably like sinking?'

'Exactly.'

'Well,' Avril said, 'Otterbury Hall seems a queer haven of refuge, especially for you.'

'I hadn't thought of it as a haven,' her sister assured her dryly, as she got up to go.

'But you'll enjoy being rich, Ismay. Even you couldn't do anything else. There'll be clothes and jewels and furs and travel—and all of it for nothing.'

'No,' Ismay said slowly. 'All of it on credit—and the bill to be paid one day.'

Avril gave her a puzzled little glance. Then she shrugged and laughed.

'Well, that's the most comfortable way of arranging things, isn't it? It's the way we've always done things. Promised to pay tomorrow. And then quite often tomorrow doesn't come.'

'I think,' Ismay said softly, 'that in Keith Otterbury's house, tomorrow follows today quite inevitably.'

Avril didn't say anything to that, and Ismay went back into the house, determined to see if her father were in a condition to be told her news, and, if so, to face the last of these family interviews while her determination held.

When she came into her father's room, it was to find him propped up in bed, and looking very much more himself than he had at any time since the reading of Great-aunt Georgina's will. At the same time, Ismay could not help noticing that there was a great deal of grey in the thick fair hair that was so like her own and Adrian's. Perhaps it had been there before, but—— One noticed these things now, and when she saw him smile in that eager, pleased way at her entrance, she felt unspeakably glad that it was good news, and not bad, which she had to impart.

'At least, I suppose one would call it good news,' thought Ismay. 'At any rate, it won't cost him anything, poor darling!'

'Well, Ismay, my dear, you see the invalid well on the way to recovery.' Father seemed to take some personal credit for this, and he lay back against his pillows, looking very picturesque and contented.

'I'm so glad.' Ismay smiled at him. 'Do you feel in a mood for a talk, Father?'

A shadow crossed his face at once, because of course poor Father could not imagine any talk that did not involve financial embarrassment.

'Why—yes, my dear, I think so. Though of course I must not tax my strength *too* much at present.' That was his attempt to raise a barrier against any news that might be frankly disastrous.

'No, of course not. But I have something to tell you that is nice and—and rather exciting. I'm engaged. I wanted to tell you just as soon as possible.'

'Engaged? But, my dear child, this is indeed news—delightful news!'

Ismay was dreadfully afraid he was getting ready his speech about fledglings leaving the nest, and as she felt much too tired and experienced now to be a fledgling, she hurried on.

'You'll be terribly surprised when you hear who it is, but——'

Father held up his really beautiful hand and·said smilingly :

'I think you ought to allow me three guesses.'

'Oh, but you'd never guess in three guesses,' Ismay assured him rather agitatedly. 'It's Keith Otterbury.'

Father's mild annoyance at being done out of his three guesses was completely swamped in his astonishment—disagreeable astonishment at that, Ismay saw plainly.

'Keith Otterbury! My dear Ismay, you can't be serious. There must be some mistake!'

Ismay didn't really see what mistake there could be. She was silent, allowing Father to digest the news in his own way.

'Dear child, I don't think I can allow this,' he said at last. 'I had never imagined myself giving one of my daughters to a man like Keith Otterbury.'

'And I never thought of giving myself to him either,' reflected Ismay crudely.

Aloud she said :

'I know there's a great deal of uncharitable talk about him, but don't you think people always gossip about anyone who behaves impulsively and unconventionally?'

Father shook his head gravely.

'It isn't only impulse and lack of convention, my dear. There are other things—— You wouldn't understand.' Glancing at him, Ismay saw that he really thought she would not. 'Ismay, isn't this all a very sudden and thoughtless decision?'

'No,' Ismay insisted. 'I—I have met him sometimes, you know. It was only quite lately, of course, that we thought seriously of getting married. But indeed, Father, I think you'd like him, if you really knew him.'

Nothing was more unlikely, Ismay felt sure, but one must at least encourage Father in the belief that his future son-in-law had some good qualities.

'He's very—kind, really,' she hurried on. 'He says he has wanted to marry me for something like two years now —ever since he first saw me.'

'Most improbable !' exclaimed Father with one of his very rare flashes of common sense. 'Nobody wants to marry a woman the first time he sees her.'

'Well,' Ismay conceded with a smile, 'I daresay that is only in a manner of speaking. But he does I—— He is very, very anxious to marry me.'

'And how about you, Ismay? Are you very much in love with him?'

'Oh—yes, of course.'

Fortunately Father put down any slight confusion on

her part to very natural and proper modesty.

'You can't imagine how generous and kind he is!' Ismay felt it was time she brought up the heavy reserves of argument. 'There is no end to the things he wants to do for me and the family.'

'Indeed?' Father looked interested : against his will.

'Oh yes. He is determined that Adrian should get his chance. He wants to—to support him during his medical training. And Avril can go to Italy and study art if she wants to. And—and Keith doesn't want us to have any more anxiety—financial anxiety, that is—in the family. He—he seems to understand so well about our difficulties, and he *really* wants to help.'

Ismay felt some astonishment herself at the convincing story she was managing to make of it all. As for Father, he listened spellbound. Whatever objections he had against Keith Otterbury as a son-in-law still existed, but undoubtedly there were some other very heavy considerations weighing down the opposite side of the scales.

'My dear Ismay! This is the most extraordinary generosity. But——' Suddenly Father recalled the sequence of events in all the best melodramas : 'All this is not in the nature of a bribe, is it? You are not—I might almost say "selling yourself"—for all these advantages, are you?' He looked anxiously at her.

'Oh no.' To tell the truth, Ismay managed to laugh, without much difficulty. 'There's nothing like that about it. I—I do love Keith, and I want to marry him. I know there are some unfortunate stories about him, but—well, I don't feel that I have a right to question his past, simply because he has asked me to share his future.'

Ismay knew that the balance of that last sentence would appeal to Father immediately. He nodded slowly and thoughtfully. It sounded admirable to his ears.

'Perhaps you are right, my dear. Perhaps you are right.'

Ismay was silent, allowing him to savour very pleasantly all the implications of what she had been saying. Now that he had admitted to himself the possibility of his daughter marrying Keith Otterbury, there was no harm in reflecting on the amazing easing of their whole position.

'You are quite sure your happiness really lies in this marriage?' he asked her once. And when she said, 'Quite sure,' she thought he looked a great deal more relieved than worried.

At last she said coaxingly:

'You haven't really any objections, Father, have you?'

'Well, child, all I want is whatever is best for you.' That was true, at any rate, Ismay knew, for Father was extremely attached to all his children. 'If you've set your heart on this marriage, and have seriously considered all it means, then it is not for me to interfere. It shall never be said of me that I influenced any of my children unduly in the choice of a husband.' He remembered Adrian then, and changed the phrase to 'in the choice of a life companion,' which sounded more impressive anyway.

Ismay saw then that he was well embarked on the stream of his own eloquence, and quite prepared to enjoy himself in the old way. It was so pleasant to see poor Father happily restored to normal that she had no difficulty in smiling attentively and murmuring agreement with all that he was saying. Only when he said, 'But I must see Keith Otterbury myself,' did she take charge of the conversation once more.

'He wants to come and see you as soon as you're well enough.'

'I am well enough now,' Father insisted firmly, and indeed he did look much brighter and more energetic.

'Well, I was going to telephone him this evening. He wanted to know when he could come and ask you formally for permission to marry me.'

'Very proper,' murmured Father, delighted with this unusual show of ceremony. 'I see no reason why he should not come this evening, Ismay. Not too late, of course. But tell him I shall be happy to receive him about seven o'clock.'

'Very well.' Ismay secretly marvelled at the attitude of pleasant condescension which Father was quite prepared to adopt towards the man who was going to pay his debts for him.

'No wonder he always got away with everything,' she reflected as she went out of the room. 'He is so honestly convinced that it's he who dispenses the favours.'

The house was very quiet when she came downstairs. Susan was not yet home from school, Avril was still out in the garden, and Adrian, she supposed, was out on some concern of his own. It was a good opportunity to telephone now to Keith Otterbury. (She would have to remember to think of him now as 'Keith'. One could not call one's fiancé by his whole name, even in one's thoughts.)

She went over to the telephone, and then had to stop to look for his number in the directory. It was queer, somehow, not even to know the telephone number of the man you were going to marry. She knew the numbers of all their other acquaintances by heart, and practically never looked inside the directory from one year's end to the other. But then, of course, Keith was not—and never had been—an acquaintance of theirs.

While she waited for him to answer, her gaze wandered absently about the hall, noting familiar details which usually hardly aroused her attention. Heavens! the place was shabby. One could hardly expect anything else, of course. Four children had been brought up in this house, and there had hardly ever been a penny for repairs or decorations.

It was difficult to remember any other wallpaper. This one had been put on in Mother's time, and that discoloured patch near the bottom of the stairs was where a two-year-old Susan had scribbled on it with a pencil, a week after it had been put up. Mother had done miracles with india-rubber and breadcrumbs, but the shadow of Susan's misdeeds still lingered.

And then that mark on the hall table. That had happened after some misguided person had given Adrian a carpentering set for Christmas. She could remember quite well——

'Hello.' The voice in her ear recalled her to the present rather sharply.

'May I speak to Mr. Otterbury, please?'

'Speaking.'

'Oh, Mr. Ott—I mean, Keith, this is Ismay speaking. I thought you would like to know that I've told the family.'

She heard him laugh.

'How did they take it?'

'Oh, they were—surprised, of course.'

'Of course.'

'But quite pleased.' And then, remembering Adrian's

expression, she added, 'On the whole.'

'A mixed reception, in fact.'

'Well, that's all you—we could expect, isn't it?'

'I suppose so.'

'Anyway, Father would like very much to see you. This evening, if possible.'

'I'll come. Does he want to express approval or disapproval?'

'Oh, I think he is pleased, on the whole. He wouldn't have *chosen* you, exactly,' she added with candour. 'But then——'

'—Nor would you?' he suggested.

'I wasn't going to say that.'

'Very well.' She heard that amused laugh again. 'I will come. About seven?'

'Yes, about seven.' And then because there was nothing else to say to him at all, she added a rather curt 'Goodbye' and rang off.

At tea-time she told the others briefly :

'Keith will be coming this evening.'

'Whatever for?' Adrian inquired, with casual rudeness. While Susan said :

'My goodness ! I must get my homework done early.'

By which Ismay gathered she did not intend to miss anything.

As seven o'clock drew near, she began to feel ridiculously nervous. And, acting on an impulse she could hardly explain, she went out of the house, and walked a little way down the lane, in the direction from which he must come.

Apparently punctuality was one of his minor virtues,

for it was still only a few minutes to seven when she heard his footsteps. The bend in the lane still hid him from her view, but she felt she was already beginning to know that long, rapid stride very well.

He was looking very serious when she first saw him, but his face lit up with a smile when he caught sight of her.

'My dear, this is very charming of you. Or is it just your first effort to show the mild devotion which I suggested might be tactful in public?'

'No. I just—felt nervous in the house, and thought I would come a little way to meet you.'

He smiled rather quizzically, and put his arm lightly round her waist, as he fell into step beside her.

'Were you nervous on my behalf, or on your own?'

'Oh—I don't know. Just over the general situation, I expect.'

He glanced down at her, as though he would say something else about that. But apparently he changed his mind, because after a moment he said quite abruptly:

'I brought you your ring, Ismay.'

'Already!' She was astonished. 'But when did you find time to get it?'

To her surprise he flushed, for the first time since she had known him.

'Perhaps I had it already,' he told her with a smile.

'But you couldn't. You had no idea that this was going to happen.'

'How do you know I haven't cherished your ring in readiness all this time—hoping that one day my luck might turn?'

In spite of his mocking tone, she glanced at him

curiously. She had the odd feeling that it was the sort of preposterous thing he might do. But she only said rather grimly :

'That would be a rather costly indulgence in sentiment, I should think.'

'Ismay, haven't you a grain of romance in your composition?' he laughed down at her accusingly.

She was silent, because she thought it was rather unreasonable to expect her to have any feeling of romance where he was concerned. Perhaps he remembered that too after a moment, because, without pursuing the subject further, he took her ring from his pocket.

He made no attempt to put it on her finger, she noticed. Only held it out in the palm of his hand, and, after a second's hesitation, she took it.

'Oh, how lovely !' The exclamation was forced from her involuntarily.

'You like it?' he was pleased. She could tell that from his tone.

'Yes, of course. It's heavenly. However did you get it?'

'I've told you,' he said teasingly. 'I have had it all this time in the hope that one day you would wear it.'

'But——' she brushed that aside. 'Where did you find it originally?'

'In a shop in Athens. It may be Greek work—I'm not sure. But it's the colour of your eyes. That's why I bought it.'

She was quite silent, gazing at the most beautiful piece of lapis lazuli she had ever seen, pretending she had not heard his last sentence.

The ring was curiously and most exquisitely wrought, the pure yellow of soft, unalloyed gold forming the perfect setting for the blue of the lapis lazuli. The value of it lay in the workmanship, and it was evidently the fine flower of some true artist's work. There was something almost barbaric about it, and Ismay thought, 'It's the kind of ring one *would* associate with Keith.'

At that moment he said, 'You can have the usual solitaire, too, if you like—or whatever you specially fancy. But that ring is essentially yours. It suits you.'

'I don't want anything else, thank you. There's nothing I could like as much as this,' Ismay told him frankly. And then, after a moment, 'Thank you, Keith. It's wonderful.'

'I'm happy if you are pleased,' was all he said, but Ismay had the curious impression that that was literally true.

She slipped his ring on her finger without another word, and they went into the house together.

'Will you see Father first?—or the rest of the family?'

'Your father.' He smiled at her in the rather subdued light of the hall, without a trace of the nervousness which she herself was feeling.

'Come along then.' She led him upstairs, thankful that Susan, for once, refrained from rushing out to inspect the newcomer on her own account.

The sonorous 'Come in,' with which Father answered her knock showed that he was prepared, in every sense, for his visitor. And as Ismay led the way into the room, she wondered very much if Keith would find Father amusing or—still worse—if he would be unkind enough to show it.

Keith's greeting, however, was as faultless as Father's own. And he did not allow himself even the slightest twinkle when—after the first few conventionalities— Father said to her :

'My dear, I think you had better leave us alone together.'

Ismay went out of the room. She would have felt faintly sorry for anyone else in the circumstances, but she thought Keith could manage the situation very well, and, even if he could not—well, that served him right for some of the horrid things he had said and done.

She didn't go downstairs again—feeling a little unwilling to face the comments and questions of the others. Instead, she went across to the bedroom which she shared with Avril, and stood by the window, staring out into the garden, slowly turning her curious and beautiful ring upon her finger.

It felt odd there. She had never worn a ring before, and this one felt unusually heavy on her hand. It was a wonderful ring, though—the kind of ring which must have taken a lot of finding. Athens—that was where he had said he bought it. Somehow that made it even more curious.

Then he *must* have bought it some while ago, for she felt sure he had not been away from the district for very long at a time during this year at least. And he had said he bought it because it was the colour of her eyes.

But that was ridiculous. He could hardly have been thinking of her eyes at that time. That was just a bit of romantic ballyhoo, which he thought sounded good. He had bought the ring because he liked it. Nothing more nor less.

She wondered what he was saying to Father now. Or rather, what Father was saying to him—because, of course, Father would see to it that he did most of the talking. He was quite capable of taking Keith to task about previous escapades, and reading him a grave and impressive lecture. She could not quite decide how Keith would take such an attack but, try as she would, she could not imagine him in any way discomfited.

Father would be very man-to-man, of course, implying that he too had been something of a dog in his day, but that there were 'limits'. It would be quite untrue, needless to say, for nothing could have been more intensely respectable in thought and deed than Father.

Whereas, with Keith—— No, 'respectable' was not the word to describe Keith.

She heard the door of Father's room open, and his musical, penetrating voice saying something ending in 'my dear boy'. That sounded as though they had reached some satisfactory agreement, and, smiling faintly, she came to the door of her room.

Keith was just coming out of Father's room, and he said over his shoulder, through the half-open door :

'She's here, sir. Would you like to speak to her now?'

(Oh, how Father would like that 'sir' ! Adrian had never called him that in spite of sundry encouragements to do so.)

'No, no.' Father's tone was geniality itself. 'I'll give her my blessing later. It's your voice that she wants to hear at the moment.'

Ismay saw the sardonic light leap up in Keith's smiling eyes. He softly closed the door and came towards her.

'How charming—but how untrue !' he said, looking down at her.

'Will you come down and meet the others now?' She spoke with studied calm.

'Don't you want to hear the result of my interview?'

'I know it,' Ismay told him. 'Father wouldn't sound so

genial or you look so cock-a-hoop if things hadn't gone smoothly.'

'So *what*? Lord! Do I really look that?' He grinned reflectively. 'Well, now I come to think of it, that is how I feel.'

'Because Father has agreed to let you pay his debts?' she said dryly, and turned away.

He came close behind her, and put his arms round her, imprisoning her lightly.

'No. Forget about your father's debts and your brother's ambitions and all the rest of it——'

'Shall I forget about Avril too?' she interrupted coolly, refusing to look round at him, though she was terribly aware of his nearness.

'Ismay, haven't you *one* kind word to say to me?'

'Why should I?'

'Because—do you really want to know?'

'Well?'

'Because I love you, you little beast.' He turned her almost roughly and kissed her on her mouth before she could stop him. 'Because I don't mind what this damned, cadging family of yours costs, so long as I have you. Because—oh God, I'm sorry! I'm saying all the wrong things, of course.'

'Well, at least—I don't much like—the way you speak of my family.' She tried very hard to make that cool and scornful, but she was terribly shaken really by his outburst, and her words came in unsteady little gasps.

'I apologise.' There was a shade of something like sullenness in his dark eyes. 'Shall we go downstairs and—meet the family, as you suggested?'

Ismay led the way without a word.

Downstairs in the drawing-room the other three members of the family were grouped in rather uneasy silence, but as soon as Ismay and Keith came in, the tension seemed broken.

Until that moment Ismay had not had time to think how awkward the greeting between Avril and Keith was almost bound to be. She had one moment of panic—and then saw that there was no need for distress on her part. They measured each other with a cool little stare, then the faintest smile crossed Avril's face, while Keith's 'How are you, Avril?' held very much more than a hint of amusement. It was extraordinary how well they did it.

Actually the meeting with Adrian was the most difficult one, because somehow Adrian refused to show any of his usual graciousness and charm. He contented himself with the curtest of greetings, and then left the field to Susan—who occupied it with alacrity.

'How d'you do? I'm Susan, and I know you very well by sight even though I haven't been introduced to you before. And do tell me, is that great black horse of yours really as wicked as it looks?'

'No,' Keith assured her coolly. 'She's like her master—has a deceptive appearance which makes people think her more wicked than she is.'

'O-oh.' Susan turned that over in her mind. 'I don't think you look very wicked,' she observed at last.

'Don't you? I'm relieved.'

Susan, however, refused to take that at its face value.

'I don't believe you a bit,' she declared cheerfully. 'You don't care a hang what I think—or what anybody else thinks either. Everyone says so.'

'Indeed? And who is "everyone"?' he wanted to know.

But Susan didn't see how one could define that more clearly. She made a vague gesture with her hand and amended her expression to, 'Oh—everybody, you know.'

'You mean I have a general reputation in the neighbourhood for not caring about anything or anyone?'

'I suppose that's it,' Susan agreed. 'Still, people can't say that now, because they'll know you must care for Ismay or you wouldn't be marrying her.'

'How do you like the idea of redeeming me in the eyes of the world, Ismay?' He turned to her with a smile.

'I think it would take more——' began Ismay sharply. Then she stopped, suddenly remembering that she had to play the part of an affectionate and happy fiancée. Somehow she contrived to summon a smile. 'I don't think there is any redemption needed. Susan always talks in an exaggerated way,' she said mildly.

'I don't!' Susan was indignant. 'And you know quite well that Father himself said——' She stopped suddenly, overcome by belated tact, and for once no one heard what it was that 'Father had said'.

Ismay found herself wondering just how much Keith was really enjoying this, for all that mocking little smile of his suggested that he found them all amusing. After all, surely no man actually *liked* to feel that people thought him a pretty shocking person.

But whatever Keith really felt, he kept his thoughts to himself, and even if the evening could hardly be considered an unqualified success, at least it was redeemed from real failure by the easy, if slightly scornful, good temper of the guest of honour.

More than once, Ismay noticed that he gave a very quizzical glance in Avril's direction, but she withstood it well, and nothing in the manner of either would have aroused the suspicions of any casual observer.

Only when they went out into the garden after supper, Ismay noticed that Keith deliberately strolled on ahead with Avril, and instinctively, she herself kept Susan and Adrian back with some inquiry about some plant in which not one of them was genuinely interested at the moment. She felt it was better that the other two should say whatever they wanted to say to each other now. It would save complications later. There could surely not be much that they could want to say to each other in the circumstances, but she could imagine that a few candid words now might well save misunderstanding and bad feeling later.

'I think he's awfully *attractive*, Ismay.' Susan seized the opportunity to give her opinion at the earliest possible moment. 'I don't believe he takes anything very seriously —but then nor does Adrian, so you'll be used to that.'

'Thank you. Just count me out of that,' her brother told her dryly. 'I don't think I've much in common with him. At least, I hope not.'

'Adrian—please.' Ismay was distressed, though she felt she was probably not showing sufficient distress for a devoted fiancée who wanted her choice of husband approved by her family.

'Sorry, my dear. But he's not my type. And to tell the truth, I can't imagine that he's yours either.'

Ismay didn't answer that, and presently they rejoined the others. As they did so, she heard Keith say:

'On the contrary, my dear Avril, I'm grateful to you. In fact, I hope you will enjoy Italy enormously, and I'll certainly do everything I can to see that you do.'

She wondered a little what reason he had for being

grateful, and decided that it was probably some relief to him that Avril had not resented his changing his attention from one sister to the other.

Then Susan introduced a rather strained note into the conversation with the leading question :

'Well, when are you going to be married? Quite soon, I suppose?'

'I think so.' Keith looked as though he were deferring to Ismay's wishes, but she already knew that the slight tightening at the corners of his mouth meant that he intended to have things his way.

'Yes. I—we don't see that there's any reason for a long engagement.' (That at least was true, for certainly the tangled family affairs would not wait for a leisurely straightening out.) 'We thought in about—— She hesitated, looking questioningly at Keith, and he finished for her quite calmly :

'In about a fortnight's time.'

Ismay gasped, for she had not thought of it all being so close upon her as that, but fortunately Susan's astonishment was sufficiently vocal to drown any sound her sister made.

'A fortnight? My goodness! You *are* in a hurry, aren't you? I can't think what Carol will say'—no one seemed greatly exercised at the thought of Carol's reactions—'she was astonished enough this afternoon when I told her you were going to get married, because, as she said, you hardly even *knew* each other, and it must have been love at first sight. But *this* I I suppose Avril and I'll be bridesmaids. What a pity you're grown up, Adrian, otherwise you could have been a page.' Adrian made a slight, inarticulate sound of horror. 'And really, a wedding is something where we *can* shine, because we shall all look awfully nice. Let's have wreaths, Avril. They're much nicer than hats. What a good job you and I are both the ones with red hair, because then we shan't quarrel over colours, because whatever suits you will suit me. Green'd be nice, wouldn't it?—and as we're none of us superstitious——'

'Is this your wedding or Ismay's?' inquired her future brother-in-law at this point.

'Oh, well, Ismay's always sweet about that sort of thing. And anyway, she's bound to wear white and she looks marvellous in white, so she can't grudge us whatever we look best in.'

'Yes, she must look marvellous in white,' was all Keith said, and for once he was not laughing.

'Oh, I don't know that there will be time to arrange a white wedding.' Ismay spoke hastily, rousing herself from abstraction and only realising with difficulty that it was her own wedding that was being discussed.

'There will be plenty of time,' Keith said. And she knew at once that what he meant was that there would be plenty of money, and wherever there was plenty of money things could be done to order.

Susan, evidently considering that this point was satisfactorily settled, proceeded a little further along a delicate path, with the cheerful inquiry :

'And then where'll you go for your honeymoon? Abroad?'

'No.' Ismay said that almost violently, because at Susan's words she suddenly saw the complete picture at last. Herself alone with Keith in some strange hotel, miles and miles away from home and everyone she knew—the last link with familiarity snapped, the last bridge back over the gulf destroyed.

For a moment she felt terribly sick, and more frightened than she would have believed possible. Why did one have to have a honeymoon at all? It would be terrible enough going home with Keith to Otterbury Hall, knowing that he was her husband, that her life belonged more or less to him henceforward. Why should she be forced to stage the first ghastly scenes in some place remote from her home and every single thing that could give her the slightest scrap of confidence?

'I don't think I want a honeymoon,' she heard herself say in a slightly strangled voice, and she looked round defiantly, feeling that now indeed she had knocked the bottom out of any pretty pretence there had ever been. As though in the distance she saw Susan's astonishment, the lift of Adrian's eyebrows, the close way Avril was watching her. Then Keith's voice said casually :

'No, I don't know that I do either. Honeymoons are always something of a mistake, I feel.'

She gave a slight gasp. The world seemed to right itself again. She was trembling a little with the sense of the nearness of disaster. But keenest of all in her thoughts at the moment was the curious certainty that Keith had understood her terror and had answered her unspoken appeal.

CHAPTER SIX

'BUT I never heard of anyone not having a honeymoon,' Susan said. 'At least, not anyone who got married, I mean.'

'Lots of people prefer to have it later,' Keith assured her, and Ismay was thankful that he took on the arguing of the matter. With anyone as positive about conventions as Susan could be, it was not a specially easy task. 'Since we're not having a long engagement,' he went on casually, 'and since Ismay wants to make as little break with her own home as possible, I don't see why we shouldn't have a quiet wedding——'

'But with bridesmaids!' Susan got that in.

'All right, with bridesmaids, if that's what Ismay wants. And then postpone our honeymoon. That will leave her free to arrange—whatever she likes for all of you. Then when we do go, we can make it a long trip if we want.'

'Something like a world tour, you mean?' Susan was beginning to see the advantages of the plan now.

Keith shrugged slightly and smiled.

'If that's what Ismay would like.'

'My goodness, Ismay! Everything is what you would like. You *are* going to have a good time,' Susan remarked frankly.

Somehow Ismay smiled slightly.

'Yes, I'm sure of that.'

But she wished Adrian would not look quite so rudely sceptical.

Very much later that evening, when Keith was finally leaving, she strolled with him to the gate. It was the only chance she had had of a word with him alone.

'Goodnight, sweetheart.' There was a curiously caressing note in his voice, but she could see, even in the moonlight, that his smile was mocking.

'Goodnight, Keith.' And then—'I want to ask you something.'

'Well?'

'Did you mean that—about our not having a honeymoon?'

'Yes. That is, if you really don't want one.'

'N—no, I'd rather not. Only why did you—bother?'

'I don't understand.' She thought the line of his chin looked faintly obstinate. 'Why did I bother about what?'

'You know quite well what I mean. Why did you bother to help me out in front of the others, when I said I didn't want a honeymoon? You could easily have forced the issue and made me accept it.'

'Do you think that would have made for an enjoyable honeymoon, Ismay?' he asked dryly.

'No, of course not. But then——' She paused helplessly, wondering what there was that could be called enjoyable about anything to do with this marriage.

He took her lightly by the arm then and smiled down at her.

'Look here, my dear, you go on thinking me the worst and most impossible fellow on earth. Then you'll have an occasional pleasant surprise when the natural beauty of my nature shows itself in a rare flash of generosity.'

She heard him laugh, and before he left her he kissed her, but lightly this time on the side of her cheek, not at all as he had kissed her before. In fact, thought Ismay, as she went slowly back into the house, that hardly counted as a kiss at all.

After that, it was difficult to say how the time slipped away so quickly. Ismay had always supposed that getting married involved a tremendous amount of arranging, but it seemed quite an astonishingly simple matter under Keith's arbitrary management. Adrian said once, rather violently, that he had a 'very offensive manner of footing the bill,' but Ismay couldn't help thinking that you either footed the bill or you didn't. And when you were paying for a lot of things which, by rights, should have been paid for by someone else, it was hard to say just what the correct manner *should* be.

'He means well. He means well,' Father declared in his most patronising manner, and nothing could have been more gracious than the way in which he was already allowing himself to be extricated from his financial swamp.

'Anyway, how should we have paid for everything ourselves?' demanded Susan with ruthless frankness. 'Ismay would simply have had to be married in any old thing she's got, because I can't imagine there is anyone left who would give us credit for so much as a handkerchief.'

'Susan, my dear, you talk a great deal too much for your age,' Father said, a trifle remotely. And, this being unquestionably true, Susan was forced to subside into silence.

On the whole, they saw little of the prospective bridegroom. Perhaps he was aware that any visits of his caused constraint rather than pleasure in the Laverhope household, or perhaps he was just busy on his own affairs. But they were aware of his hand in almost everything—and, to tell the truth, it was usually a hand that was paying out money.

'I'm afraid marrying me is proving rather an expensive luxury, Keith,' Ismay said to him dryly once. But he only replied rather curtly :

'Perhaps I consider it cheap at the price.'

That really didn't leave much more to be said on the subject, Ismay thought.

The only one who was probably wholeheartedly enjoying all the preparations was Susan. She was an insensitive child and had an enormous capacity for enjoying things which left other people squirming. But she also took the most genuine pleasure in what she supposed to be her sister's happiness.

'You're really frightfully lucky, Ismay, aren't you?' she said, when Ismay's wedding dress had been sent home and duly inspected. 'I shouldn't think many girls marry men with so much money to throw about. Or if they do, the men turn out to be mean and want to spend it all on themselves. You must be *terribly* happy.'

'Yes,' Ismay agreed—inadequately, she felt, but it was difficult to bubble with enthusiasm in the circumstances.

'It was funny he should have been in love with you and all the time we imagined it was Avril.'

'Very funny,' Ismay said, and then thought the word was singularly ill-chosen.

She could not decide what to make of Avril these days. Apparently she was perfectly willing to take casual pleasure in the preparations for her sister's wedding, just exactly as though she herself had had nothing to do with Keith.

'I don't see how anyone could come to such an enormous decision as Avril, and then coolly drop the whole idea, as though it had never existed,' thought Ismay. But then, she reflected, not for the first time, Avril was an entirely inexplicable person.

Sometimes, lately, she thought perhaps she herself was rather an inexplicable person. She had always supposed that she would let her life run in uneventful, conventional channels. Although warmly affectionate, she had never thought of herself as indulging in violent emotional storms, or involving herself in situations where anger and fear and hate waited just round the corner.

She tried not to think too much of the way Keith had kissed her, that time outside Father's room. But if that had meant anything at all, it had meant that he had some sort of violent passion for her. And, that being so, what was it going to be like when he had the ordering of her life for her?

'If there were *any* way out I would take it,' Ismay thought. But there was no way out. At least, none that she could find.

She was still seeking vainly for it when her wedding day arrived.

There was no denying the fact—as Susan had said—a wedding was the kind of occasion on which the Laverhopes could hardly help distinguishing themselves. If only it had been someone else's wedding, Ismay could have enjoyed it intensely, because it was fun to know that the whole family looked simply wonderful. She could not feel impatient even with the garrulous jubilation of Susan, because it was natural enough. But it made her a little faint to remember that, when all this charming pageant was over, she would no longer be Ismay Laverhope, living a careless, hand-to-mouth, but somehow enjoyable existence. She would be Keith Otterbury's wife—with an enormous bill to pay in one form or another.

She wondered how many people guessed the real situation as she came down the aisle on Father's arm. Very few, she supposed, because there was not the faintest shadow of compulsion in the gracious air with which Father was about to bestow his daughter upon the faintly smiling, arrogant man who waited so coolly for them near the chancel steps.

A hint of it might have been gleaned from the rather set look on Adrian's handsome young face, but the afternoon sunshine through the stained-glass window over the altar was kind to Adrian. It imparted a soft radiance to his thick fair hair and mellowed the grim line of his mouth, so that he looked like a very serious angel, watching his sister intently in this most important moment of her life.

'Dearly beloved——'

The service had begun, with perhaps the most incongruous words it was possible to use, in the circumstances.

Ismay was very calm—so calm that she was a little surprised at herself. She noticed that her voice was as steady as Keith's when she had to speak, and if the pitch was low, there was nothing unusual in that because Father (backed by no less authority than King Lear) had always insisted that this was 'an excellent thing in women.'

It was over at last, and in the vestry Father was kissing her on the forehead—which he considered appropriate but everyone else thought somewhat unnatural—and saying, 'My dear child, this is a very happy moment for us all.'

Ismay was glad that someone honestly thought so, and,

so far as she could tell from the expressions around her, she gave an excellent impression herself of being a very happy bride.

When she and Keith came out of the church into the sunlight, it seemed that most of the people who had known her all her life were gathered there to throw confetti at her, wish her well, and see if her wedding dress suited her.

They had also come to gaze with somewhat pleasurable disapproval at the man she had chosen for her husband.

Well, there he was! Settled down at last. And if anyone had a chance of taming him that pretty Ismay Laverhope had. But really, one never *knew*.

It was only a few moments' drive from the church to the one hotel in the place which possessed a room suitable for a wedding reception, and on the way they were both strangely silent.

Just once he picked up her hand as it lay slackly on her knee, and looked at the thin gold band on it.

'What is it?' She spoke very quietly.

'Nothing.' He let her hand go. 'I'm trying to believe it's true, that's all.'

She wondered if he knew she was trying to believe it was *not* true. But they arrived at the hotel without her saying any more. And two or three minutes later they were smilingly greeting their guests as though this were the happiest day of their lives.

Later Ismay wondered if she need really have made such a point of not wanting to go on a honeymoon. At least it would have meant some sort of a break—some novelty to take her thoughts from her strange and terrible situation. As it was, when everything was over, she drove home with Keith to Otterbury Hall, feeling tired and bewildered, but quite shockingly unmarried. It seemed even faintly ridiculous that the car should keep straight on down the road to the Hall, instead of turning off by the familiar way that would have taken her really 'home'. The Hall seemed nothing but a strange house when she reached it.

'Tired?' Keith lifted her out of the car and set her lightly on the ground.

'Yes, I am a bit. I suppose it's rather a strain.'

'I expect so. We'll have a quiet evening. Now I really do applaud your wisdom in ruling out a honeymoon. I can't imagine anything better calculated to make us loathe each other than to have to start off on a long railway journey feeling like this.'

Ismay thought that *she* could imagine other things better calculated to make her loathe him, but they were not the sort of things one put into words. Only, in the moment that she entered the house, the grim reality of what she had taken on seemed to become terribly dark and clear-cut. It was like hearing the rattle of the first stones that heralded the fall of an avalanche. One could not do anything about it. One could only wait helplessly.

The housekeeper was in the hall waiting to take her to her room, and something about that made Ismay think :

'How impersonal Keith's life is. There is absolutely no one who seems to belong to him. Only excellent servants who do all the things he wants. I wonder if his family just won't have anything to do with him.'

One could not ask that outright, of course, but she thought she would make some sort of inquiry when she came downstairs again.

The room into which the housekeeper showed her was

large and full of evening sunshine. There were windows on two sides which gave an effect of space and light, and the furniture, though neither modern nor definitely antique, had an indefinable air of elegance which gave the room character and charm. The carpet and the hangings were blue, and across one end of the room stretched an enormous white bearskin rug.

'Oh, what a nice room! I like it,' Ismay exclaimed involuntarily, and the housekeeper immediately smiled and said:

'Yes, I always think it the nicest room in the house. I'm very glad to see it used again, madam. It was last used by Mr. Otterbury's mother, you know. That's her portrait over there.'

Ismay crossed the room, and examined the portrait of Keith's mother with some interest.

'She's very like him.' She spoke without looking round.

'Ye—es.' There was some doubt in the housekeeper's tone. 'She was not at all like him in disposition.'

'Wasn't she?' Ismay wondered very much what that meant, but no further information seemed forthcoming. She gazed for a moment longer at the slightly haughty, oval face, set with such fine dark eyes. She even had Keith's faintly mocking smile. Or rather—no, there was the difference, Ismay realised suddenly. She had never seen Keith smile without the sparkle reaching his eyes. The eyes of the woman in the portrait were completely unsmiling.

'Is there anything you would like, madam?'

Ismay turned back into the room.

'No, thank you. I'll change right away and come downstairs. Is this the door through into the bathroom?' She crossed the room.

'Yes, madam. And that door leads into Mr. Otterbury's room.'

When the housekeeper had gone, Ismay looked slowly round the room. So that door led into Mr. Otterbury's room, did it? And quite understandable too, since Mr. Otterbury was her husband.

A quarter of an hour later Ismay came downstairs again. She first tried the room where she had been on that evening she came to see Keith, and found that open french windows led from there on to the lawn, and that Keith was already out there, talking to the gardener.

As she stood a little doubtfully in the doorway, he looked up and saw her, and, dismissing the gardener with a word or two, he came towards her.

'Hello. Are you coming out here for ten minutes while the light still lasts?'

Ismay came out to him, and said at once:

'I like my room. I think it's beautiful.'

'Do you?' He smiled. 'I didn't have anything altered because I thought you would probably like to decide on any changes yourself.'

'But I don't think I shall want anything changed.'

'No? But I thought the only personal pleasure you expected from your aunt's money was going to be the fun of having the house re-done.'

'But that was at *home*. That's quite different. There was so much that needed doing there that it would have been nice to have it done. But here—I don't quite know how I could improve on my room.'

'I see. Well, if you do want to alter anything, you can, you know.'

'Thank you. But I think I like it as your mother had it. I hear it was her room when she lived here.'

'Yes.'

'She must have been a very beautiful woman, judging from her portrait.'

'Yes, she was. That portrait is extremely like her.'

Ismay glanced at him then and asked :

'Haven't you any family left at all, Keith?'

'No.'

'You were the only child?'

'Yes.'

'And your parents are both dead?'

'Several years ago.'

'That's rotten.'

'What is?'

'Oh—having no family life, I suppose I meant. It's almost the nicest thing there is. At least, I think so. That's why an only child is a mistake.'

He looked at her quizzically and said :

'I'm glad you think so. I agree.' And when she flushed at that he was horrid enough to laugh. He also added, quite deliberately, 'I shouldn't like any child of mine to be an only child.'

She wondered what on earth she was expected to say to that. After a moment she asked, with an effort :

'Were you unhappy as a child, then?'

'Only, sometimes. At others, I enjoyed myself healthily, like all young animals. But only children are very apt to fix their thoughts and affections on one person—usually some one who is indifferent to them. They don't mix enough with their own kind to get a right proportion on these things.'

125

'Do they—grow out of it?' Ismay asked that with a sidelong glance at him that was not without humour.

'The tendency, you mean? No, my cruel little Ismay, I rather think they don't.' He took her lightly by the arm, and fell into step beside her. 'That's why they sometimes proceed to quite fantastic and absurd lengths to get what they want.'

'I see. And who was the object of your adoration when you were a child?—Your mother?'

'Yes.'

'But she liked that? She wasn't indifferent, surely?'

'Oh, very. She was not a maternal kind of woman at all. Besides, she thought me a self-assertive, tiresome brat —which I probably was.'

'It certainly sounds in character,' Ismay agreed, again with that hint of a smile.

There was a slight silence. Then he said quite seriously, 'Do you think me self-assertive and tiresome?'

'Do you want me to answer that seriously?'

'I think so—yes.'

'Well, you've never struck me as exactly retiring,' Ismay told him dryly.

She thought he would laugh at that. He did—but a little vexedly.

'Horrible development of a horrible child, eh?'

'I didn't say that. Besides, I don't expect you were a horrible child at all. Very few children are really that. Anyway, your mother ought to have noticed you a bit. All children like to show off—it's only natural. They should be allowed to, so long as they don't overdo it.'

'Ismay,' he said softly, 'you are removing quite a number of my fears in connection with you.'

'I don't think you're the slightest bit afraid of me,' Ismay retorted, feeling that the shoe was on the other foot. 'And, anyway, there are a lot of things one can excuse in a child which one doesn't like in a man.'

'I'll try to remember that.' He was laughing again, she saw.

'What did you do to make your mother notice you?' she asked, after a moment. 'Work hard at school and bring home good reports?'

'Ismay, you know perfectly well that I couldn't possibly have been that sort of child. No, I didn't do anything constructive, I suppose. I imagined all sorts of dramatic scenes in which I rescued her from wild bulls and other improbable animals——'

'Poor little boy!' Ismay laughed softly. 'And then everyone was to hail you as a hero?'

'That was the general idea, I've no doubt.'

'And did anyone ever hail you as a hero?'

'Oh no. On the contrary, most people recognised me for what I was—a damned little pest.'

'*So* bad?'

'I'm afraid so. I suppose I thought it was better to be an *enfant terrible* than to be ignored.'

'And the step from the *enfant terrible* to the black sheep of the family is just one of natural development?' she said slowly.

'Ismay'—he laughed slightly—'I wonder if you know how adorable you are when you speak in that very grim tone, but show that understanding little dimple in your cheek.'

She didn't answer that, but suddenly she turned her head and looked him full in the face.

'Did you ever think of rescuing *me* from wild bulls?' she inquired, with cool interest.

'I—not exactly.' He was smiling still, but, for a wonder, those bold eyes of his fell. 'There are other things, besides bulls,' he murmured, with a touch of real confusion.

'I think you're very silly,' Ismay said severely, but, acting on an impulse she could never afterwards explain, she bent forward and kissed his cheek.

'Ismay!' His rather extravagant lashes swept up and he looked very startled. 'What is that for?'

'I don't really know,' she admitted. 'Except that I suppose debts and despair could be reckoned as wild bulls, for the purposes of argument. Shall we go in now?'

So they went indoors, and he said nothing more at all about her kissing him. And if once or twice during dinner he glanced at her with a faintly puzzled expression—well, there was more than enough in all of this to puzzle anyone.

He took her round the house after dinner, showing her the things which he himself liked best.

'It's an attractive house, in a rambling way,' Ismay said.

'I like it. I was hoping you would like it well enough not to want to live in London very much.'

'Oh, I don't want to live in London.' Ismay looked surprised. 'This feels much more like home.' Then she added curiously, 'But if I *had* wanted to, would you have been prepared to change?'

'You can have your way in most things,' he told her with a smile which had a hint of grimness about it.

And Ismay wondered very much which were the things which 'most' did not cover.

She wondered again—with even more point—later that

evening when she was undressing in her beautiful blue bedroom.

It seemed to her now that at *some* point in their brief and unusual engagement she ought to have found out on just what terms he expected them to live when they were married. But there had never been the faintest opportunity—or else it was that she had instinctively winced away from the kind of reply she would probably have received.

Even now she could imagine him saying in that horrid, mocking way of his, 'I told you I've wanted you for two years. What sort of terms were you expecting?'

She wished her heart wouldn't beat so hard or her mouth feel so dry. After all, it was she, so far, who had received everything in this bargain. It was pretty poor-spirited of her to feel now that she so desperately wanted to call the whole thing off. Anyway, it was too late, of course. Much, much too late.

She could hear him moving about in the room next door. He even whistled softly once or twice, which she thought disgustingly unconcerned of him. But she supposed he had reason to feel high-spirited. There must be a good deal of triumph for him in the present situation. Two years! It was a long time. Only—she had forgotten —that was probably only a boast of his, and had no foundation in truth.

Ismay got into bed. And as she did so, she heard him knock on the door between their rooms.

For a moment her throat muscles refused to obey her effort to speak. Then she said, 'Come in,' and watched the door open.

He looked fantastically handsome in his dark silk dressing-gown, which ought, somehow, to have been reassuring. But it was not reassuring in the least. Ismay knew that her eyes widened to their fullest extent, and that she watched him every inch of the way across the room. She tried to make her expression natural, but it was impossible, and she was not specially surprised when he leant his arms on the end of the bed, and raised one eyebrow in an extremely quizzical fashion.

'My dear, am I such an altogether terrifying sight?'

Ismay glanced down, plucking nervously at the sheet with her finger and thumb. She said 'No,' but the word meant nothing at all.

'What is the matter, then?'

'You know quite well what is the matter.'

'Ismay, my dear,' he spoke dryly, 'after all, I have married you.'

She glanced up quickly then, and fear and anger drove her into speech.

'You're the kind of man who would say to a slave, "After all, I have *paid* for you"—and then you'd beat him to death for your own pleasure.'

There was a strange and ragged silence. Then he said quietly :

'Is that really the impression I give you?'

She nodded, but looked away from him.

He didn't move. He just said, still in the same quiet voice :

'What do you suggest I should do, then?'

'I—don't know.' Her voice seemed to stick in her throat with nervousness.

'But I should like to hear what you consider the—right

thing in the circumstances. Do I just say "goodnight" politely and retire decorously to my room—to live a bachelor existence, enlivened from time to time by a sight of you across the breakfast-table?'

She looked at him helplessly, wordless with dismay.

'Speak to me, Ismay. Say something. I want to know what's going on behind those angry eyes of yours.'

'They're not—angry. They're frightened,' she gasped. 'I don't know what to say to you. I only thought—I only thought——'

'Yes?'

'Keith, why can't you give me time? What you're asking me to do is something that isn't easy even with a man one—knows and—loves. I don't know you. I don't love you. I'm hardly used to the idea that I've left my home and my familiar life for you. In theory I've agreed to do this thing. In practice—in practice—— Keith, won't you please wait—give me time? Not—tonight.'

She saw him straighten up slowly, his eyes singularly bright and hard.

'My God!' he said with dangerous pleasantness. 'The old, old Laverhope story. Pay me tomorrow, eh?'

And without another word, he turned and went out of the room.

CHAPTER SEVEN

ISMAY awoke next morning to a sense of disaster only just avoided. As her thoughts cleared a little more, she wondered if disaster had indeed been avoided, or whether to feel ashamed and unhappy like this was not the worst disaster that could happen to anyone.

Even now she moved uneasily at the memory of Keith's last words to her. There was some dreadful sort of truth in them, of course, argue how you would.

Oh yes, it had been a monstrous bargain. And oh yes, she had acted under something as near compulsion as made no difference. But she *had made the bargain*. And then—somehow—she had wriggled out of it.

'But I don't think I consciously meant to,' Ismay thought distractedly. 'It was only that—I was afraid, and I said what I thought—and—he went. Why didn't I make myself understood better? He thinks I'm a pretty cheat—and I know I'm a miserable coward, and—oh well, it isn't very nice, whichever way you look at it.'

She thought, when she was dressing, that she would say something about it to him at breakfast-time. She would try to make him understand that she had honestly meant she would do her best in this marriage. Only if he would give her time—oh dear, she had said that before, of course, and he had retorted with that hateful, mocking phrase that made one feel like a defaulting debtor.

On the whole, perhaps it was better to say nothing. Simply to wait, and see if an opportunity for more friendly discussion came up.

When she found how exceedingly cool and polite he was at breakfast-time, she decided more earnestly than ever in favour of avoiding thorny subjects.

It was a strangely uneventful day, considering that it was the first of their married life together. He showed her over part of the estate, rather as though she were a visitor, and, in all his explanations, she detected hardly any hint of the mocking amusement which was so characteristic of him.

For her part, she tried hard to be interested and friendly. At the bottom of her heart was a sense of something like guilt and failure. She felt she had not come out of this business with credit—either in his eyes or her own —and she was anxious to do something that would make up for the unfortunate beginning.

Late in the afternoon Susan presented herself, and never had Ismay been more glad to see her garrulous little sister. Conversation might take unexpected turns when Susan was there, but at least it never stopped dead, and Ismay felt she was just what was needed to ease the polite constraint which had existed all day between herself and Keith.

'Hello. You haven't taken long to look us up, have you?' was Keith's greeting. But Ismay thought that he too was not averse to having a third person there. And, in an amused way, he liked Susan best of her relations.

'Well, I thought you'd probably be glad to see me,' Susan explained with touching confidence. 'Besides, there isn't anything specially nice for tea at home, so I thought I'd call in here on my way back from school, and gossip about the wedding. I didn't get a chance to talk to you properly yesterday, Ismay—but wasn't it all fun?'

'Yes. It was a lovely wedding.' Ismay felt she could say that with truth.

'You looked marvellous, and I thought we did too.'

'Did you spare a glance for me?' Keith wanted to know. 'I had made a certain amount of effort with my appearance.'

'Oh yes, you looked splendid,' Susan assured him generously. 'And you were an excellent contrast to Adrian. He looked angelic, didn't he, Ismay? Adrian, I mean.'

'Thanks for the implication. I presume that, in happy contrast, I looked something like Lucifer?'

Susan regarded him thoughtfully.

'Well, you did, as a matter of fact. You needn't be offended. I always think Lucifer is the most interesting character in *Paradise Lost*.'

'An extremely unlovable character nevertheless,' Keith pointed out.

'Oh well, I don't know about that. I shouldn't press the comparison too far,' Susan said comfortably. 'And anyway if Ismay loves you, what more do you want?'

'To be sure. I hadn't thought of it that way,' Keith replied gravely.

Ismay laughed—more nervously than she had intended —and changed the subject.

'You did your part beautifully, Susan. Took my bouquet very neatly and never fidgeted once.'

'Oh, but I didn't *want* to fidget,' Susan assured her. 'I was spellbound. It was all very interesting. I'd forgotten the marriage service was quite so outspoken though, to tell the truth. It seems a bit thick talking about the children before you've got the wedding ring on. But then the

Bible and the Prayer Book always are a bit outspoken.'

Neither of her hearers appeared to have anything to say about this lapse of taste on the part of the Prayer Book.

'Still, you're sure to have lovely babies, Ismay—the kind one could mention any time, so I daresay it doesn't really matter,' Susan concluded tolerantly.

'No doubt you're right,' Keith agreed, but whether that was in answer to the first part of the remark or the second, it was impossible to say.

Susan ate a large tea and seemed very happy. She asked Keith a great many questions, which he appeared good-naturedly willing to answer, and she finally summed up flatteringly with :

'You know, you're really not much like what people say you are.'

'Let me see—what was that? Uncaring about every-thing and everyone, wasn't it?'

'Oh, I didn't mean that part so much.' Susan stared at him in the rather disconcerting way she had when her thoughts were very busy. 'I meant—about your being a very shocking person, and all that sort of thing. It's funny —even we thought you were.'

'Thought I was what?—shocking?'

'Yes. At least I know I did, and Father too. And Avril must have thought you simply the outer edge. It doesn't matter telling you now, because you're sort of part of the family, but she actually thought you were the kind of person who would take her off to the Continent if she just said the word.'

There was suddenly something very tense about the atmosphere, as though both her hearers had stopped breathing for a moment. But Susan was not at all susceptible to these shades of meaning, and she forged on quite happily.

'Honestly, I thought she meant it, the first time she said something about it. In fact, I thought you'd done everything except buy the tickets. But Avril's like that, you know. She works something out all dreamily to herself and thinks it's as good as done. She imagined she'd only got to wiggle her little finger, and you'd make all sorts of wicked proposals. And then she'd say, "Well, only in Italy," and you'd say, "All right." And there would be her precious artistic training all for nothing. She had it all worked out.' Susan paused, either to take breath or generously to allow the other two an opportunity of comment.

But neither of them seemed to have a word to say. They seemed only able to listen, in fascinated silence. And Susan, who seldom had such an attentive audience, seized the moment while it was hers.

'Of course I was simply *horrified*, and I said, "Look here, Avril Laverhope, do you mean you've talked over such a thing with a strange man?" (because after all, you were nearly a stranger then). And Avril hedged about— you know the way she does, Ismay—but I pinned her down in the end, and of course she just had to admit that she hadn't done a thing about it really, only she was quite sure she *could* if she decided to. It was a jolly good thing she *hadn't* said anything—now that we know you're different, Keith. My goodness, what on earth would you have done if she *had* suggested to you that you should go off to Italy together?' And Susan went off into peals of laughter at the thought of any *faux pas* not of her own making.

'I don't know,' Keith said mechanically, and anyone

136

more observant than Susan might have wondered why he looked so pale and bleak.

'Susan,' Ismay spoke softly, but with a peculiarly arresting note in her voice, 'what did Avril say exactly?'

Keith made a very slight movement, but neither of them took any notice.

'When?' Susan had never had so much attention paid to her lightest word, and she was puzzled as well as gratified.

'When you—pinned her down. When she—said there was really nothing in it.'

'Oh—she said, "Don't be a little fathead——" (you know the way she talks), "there's nothing to get excited about yet. I haven't said anything to him, and perhaps I never shall. But that's what I shall do if there's no other way at all." I'm not sure whether she *would*, but—— Why, Ismay, you haven't been *worrying* about it, have you?—about that word or two I said to you the day Great-aunt Georgina died. Why, of *course*—I never thought—that was why you were so upset—because you wanted Keith yourself.' Susan's expressions were always forceful rather than graceful. 'But you needn't have bothered at *all*, Ismay. I found out almost right away that there was nothing in it. I wish I'd told you then. But anyway, what a good thing I mentioned it now.'

'There is such a thing as speaking at the right time or else for ever after holding your peace,' Keith reminded her with extreme grimness. 'You don't seem to have followed either course with great success.'

'I don't know what you mean,' Susan said indignantly. 'And anyway, I expect Ismay would rather know now than not at all. Wouldn't you, Ismay?'

'Yes,' Ismay agreed quietly. 'It's better to know now than not at all.'

Keith gave an impatient little exclamation and turned away. And Susan, perceiving that, for some reason, her discourse no longer held the attention of her audience, decided that it was time to go home.

Ismay walked with her down the drive, unable to hide from her that things were not quite as they should be.

'You don't think Keith was mad at being told about Avril, do you?' Susan inquired with genuine anxiety.

'No, I don't think so.'

'I thought it was rather amusing.'

Ismay said nothing, perhaps reflecting on the peculiar gulf there was between different senses of humour.

'You aren't specially cross either, are you?' Susan wanted to know.

'No. I'm glad to know the truth.'

'You don't look specially glad,' Susan remarked frankly.

'Perhaps I was thinking that Avril might have been a little more—open with me.'

'Oh, she never is, you know. At least, I mean she never opens up naturally. You have to take a tin-opener to her. And then she won't tell you if she thinks things will turn out nicer for her by keeping silent.'

Ismay reflected, not for the first time, that there were sometimes extraordinary gleams of shrewdness buried beneath the general mass of Susan's usually uninspired conversation. No truer—if harsh—verdict had ever been passed on Avril. She would always keep silent if she thought by so doing she would make things pleasanter for herself.

'I'll come again soon, shall I?' Susan suggested as she

138

said good-bye. She made no attempt to kiss Ismay because that was not her way, but she obviously intended to give nothing but pleasure by her visits.

'Yes, come again soon,' Ismay told her, smiling a little as she turned back again towards the house.

She went in, through the french windows, to the room where she had first seen Keith. He was standing there now, his hands thrust deep in his pockets, his face set and a little expressionless.

Ismay had never before in her life wanted to hurt anyone deliberately, but she wanted to hurt him now. She looked across at him and spoke with almost casual contempt.

'And you tried to imply last night that *I* was a cheat!'
He moved then, rather sharply.

'Ismay——' he began, and then stopped.

'Yes?'

'Oh, there's nothing to say.' He shrugged helplessly. 'Except——'

'Except that you are a liar and a cheat,' she told him quietly. 'You married me on false pretences, bluffed me into taking a step I hated. I can't help wondering what you think there is to be said in your defence.'

'Nothing, except that I love you,' he said doggedly.

'I don't think you're calling things by quite their right names, Keith.'

'Nor are you,' he retorted, stung. 'You talk about my marrying you on false pretences. As a matter of fact you married me for my money, and there was damned little pretence about it.'

She was queerly silent, and after a moment he said:

'Oh, lord! I'm sorry. Don't let's sling reproaches at each

other like this. There's not much left to spoil, I know. But it's not very nice to hear the last fragments smashing. I know I did an abominable thing. I know it's pretty well past excusing. But if ever a girl handed a man temptation on a silver plate, you handed it to me that evening you came here.'

She turned to look at him with proud, angry eyes.

'I came to ask you for help—to appeal to your generosity. And you call that tempting you?'

'On the contrary, my dear,' he said—and even then there was a faint gleam of humour in his eyes—'you came to inform the bad man of the district that he was about to have an affair with your sister—the first he had heard of it—and you wanted to know whether—abandoned though he was—he could be persuaded to hold his hand.'

'Oh, it doesn't matter how you put it,' she cried impatiently. 'I was in your hands—or I thought I was. It's all the same. And you exploited my fear of what might happen to Avril. It was unpardonable—absolutely unpardonable.'

'Very well, it *is* unpardonable. Or it would be if that were the whole story. But, if you will bother to remember, Ismay, you refused those terms, as they stood. I think you even wondered if they had ever been seriously offered. It was not until we came to the point of how badly your family needed my money that you decided to make a bargain with me. I don't say that was specially noble of me either. Buying up a girl isn't a very pretty transaction. But then I didn't think it was going to be quite like that. I thought——'

'What did you think?' she asked sharply, as he hesitated.

'Oh—nothing. It doesn't matter now. I could hardly have been further out in my calculations.' And he sat down rather wearily, and for a moment he put his head in his hands.

'You thought I was going to fall into your arms, I suppose, because you'd been stuffing some of your surplus banknotes into the family's pockets?' She turned away with a little exclamation of contempt.

'No—— Ismay, don't go like that.' He caught at a fold of her dress, detaining her as a child might have done. Only she was too angry to notice that. 'Please listen to me a moment.'

'I've been listening a long time,' Ismay said. But she stood where she was, looking down into his sullen, troubled eyes. 'What is it?'

He dropped his eyes, and she saw the sullenness deepen.

'You always laugh or grow angry if I tell you that I've loved you almost since the first moment I saw you. But it's true enough. These things happen sometimes. You were so bright and fair and gentle—I'd never seen anything like you. I watched you with your family that first time and I was fascinated. They amused you so much, and yet you were so tolerant with them—so fond of them. I thought how strange it must be to live inside the magic circle of so much understanding.'

She was softened a little, in spite of herself, but she only said quietly :

'And so you decided to—push your way in.'

'No, I didn't decide anything at all at that moment. You weren't my kind—you and your family. In fact, even when I was introduced to you, your father came up and pretty openly took you away. I thought I was amused. I *was* amused—but it stung a bit too. It was quite obvious that I was never going to see you from anything but a distance.'

Ismay looked down at those strong, nervous fingers which still held a fold of her dress.

'You're not going to tell me that you went away and grieved about me in secret, are you? It's rather difficult to believe in an undying passion built on absolutely nothing.'

'No, of course it wasn't quite like that. For one thing I never really expected to be anything in your life. And for another I laughed at myself for the idea that I should remain faithful to one woman—and that one a woman who never thought twice about me——'

'But you didn't, did you?'

'Didn't what?'

'Remain faithful to me—to your ideal—whatever you like to call it. From all accounts you managed to forget me very thoroughly from time to time.'

'I tried to forget you,' he corrected her rather sombrely. 'And I accepted the fact that you never could be anything in my life. I don't know now if I ever did forget you, Ismay—it's hard to say. But I have the feeling that, in a subtle, smiling way, you always haunted me. You used to turn up in my thoughts in the most unaccountable places. Like the time I bought that ring in Athens. It was true that I bought it because it was the colour of your eyes. I never actually thought, "One day I shall give it to her." I only thought, "It's like her eyes. I must have it." '

'But you only saw me two or three times in all that while.' Ismay hardly knew whether to be touched or irritated—to believe him or to thrust his protestations back in his teeth.

'No, oftener than that, though hardly ever to speak to. I spoke to you at the County Ball, if you remember, and asked you to dance with me, but you refused.'

'I had all the dances already booked,' Ismay said hastily.

'*All* of them, Ismay?' He smiled faintly, but with real amusement.

'Yes—really all of them. But I was glad to be able to say so,' she admitted, also with the faintest smile.

'I see. Well, that was how things were, Ismay. And that was how I always expected them to be—until you walked in here that evening and informed me, free, gratis, and for nothing, that I had some sort of hold over you. It was astounding, intoxicating. It was even—forgive me, Ismay —a little amusing, to be informed that I held all the trumps, when I had never imagined myself even taking a hand in this particular game. I think it was more bravado than anything else that made me put that melodramatic offer to you. I wanted really to make some extravagantly generous gesture—but there was no gesture to make. I hadn't really got you or your sister or anyone else in my power. I couldn't magnificently put things right, because they were not even wrong. Will you be very angry if I tell you that that too amused me?'

'No, I'm not angry,' Ismay said slowly. 'At least not about that. I'm only surprised that you didn't think me a fool, and find yourself cured of this—this infatuation.'

'Cured?' He laughed slightly. 'Why, no, Ismay, I'm afraid, on the contrary, I became a fatal case. I was drunk with the indulgence of having had you to speak to for a whole evening. When you told me about the troubles in your family I wanted to assure you that I would solve

143

them all——'

'At a price.'

'It had to be some sort of practical arrangement. What do you suppose you would have done if I had just insanely offered you as much money as you liked for the asking?'

'I don't know,' Ismay said honestly. 'I suppose I should just have said "no" very quickly, and gone home thinking you a most peculiar person.'

'And that would have been the end. As it was, I suggested something that was bound to keep me in your mind. I hardly knew myself if I meant it seriously—I had some vague idea that, later, I could make the grand gesture—offer to do it all for nothing, or something of the sort. But at least the connection was there. I hadn't cut it clean off with the stunning information that I had nothing to do with your sister and had no intention of having anything to do with her.'

'It was a rotten deception, Keith, whichever way you like to look at it,' Ismay said gravely. 'You told me——'

'No, darling, I didn't tell you anything,' he reminded her gently. 'It was you who told me all about it.' And for a moment that faint smile appeared again.

'Well, it's the same thing. You let me think what was not true.'

'I know.' He sighed impatiently. 'I can't tell you now how far I intended it to be a deception and how far it was irresistibly amusing. But when you came next day and told me you were willing to marry me, it was as though the whole thing passed out of my control. I supposed you would hear the truth then from Avril, but I convinced myself that the money would be enough in itself to per-

suade you. I'm not quite sure now why Avril kept silent,
but——'

'Because she *wanted* me to marry you. She knew that
was the way to make sure of her own plans. You see, it
suited everyone that I should marry you. That was why
no one raised a hand against it,' Ismay said slowly. 'You
said something just now about a magic circle. There *was*
a circle round me—the circle of my own family. That was
why I couldn't escape.'

'Ismay!'

'I was happy in it until you forced your way in. It had
always been something very intangible—very elastic,
because it contained nothing but the family and their
common wishes. We had never pulled against each other
before. You changed all that.'

He stared up at her wordlessly—very white, with something curiously like fear in his eyes.

'You were a little jealous of that circle, weren't you,
Keith?—because you stood outside it. No one asked you
in, so you forced your way in, with a proposition that
turned us all against each other. Oh, not literally, of
course. We were just as good friends as ever on the surface.
But the good of one was no longer the good of all. It was
to the advantage of all of them that I should marry you,
whether I liked it or not. They would never have pressed
me, of course—they hadn't even a clear idea of what was
happening. But you hadn't a chance of losing, because you
had carried the war right into the—circle. You used my
family, whom I loved, as a means of putting pressure on
me. You won, of course. But you spoilt everything.'

'No—please don't say that.' He spoke violently.

145

'But it's true, isn't it? There isn't anything else to say.'
He was absolutely silent.

'May I go now?'

'Yes—of course,' he said, rather dully.

'You still have hold of my dress.'

'Oh—darling,' he exclaimed almost incoherently, and for a moment he put his face down against the fold of her dress.

Ismay looked down at his bent head, with the rather untidy dark hair.

'It wasn't quite truthful of me to insist that it was the thought of Avril which finally persuaded me,' she said slowly. 'It was the money really.'

'Oh, Ismay'—he looked up quickly—'it's very generous of you to say that now.'

'No. I think we want the exact truth at last. And the truth is that we made a bargain, you and I—that you would pay for everything my family wanted, and I would be your wife in every sense of the word.' He stiffened suddenly. 'It was just—business. You were quite right last night to be angry when I—defaulted——'

'No!'

'I ought to have remembered how much you had already paid for Father.'

'Ismay—please!'

'You said you supposed I would pay you tomorrow, but you didn't really believe it. Well, I will. I'll pay you to-night.'

'No—I don't want that,' he exclaimed violently.

'But you do. That's why you married me.'

'Oh no——'

'Yes. You even said so. Don't you remember? You said,

146

"After all, I have married you." '

'Oh, God! Did I really say that? How terrible!' He was on his feet now, trembling a little with agitation.

'Yes. And you meant it. It was all in the bargain.'

'Ismay, I beg you, don't talk any more about bargaining.'

'But I'm already most horribly in your debt on Father's account. How else do you suppose I'm going to pay?'

'You're not in my debt. Don't think any more about what I paid for your father. It's wiped off, if you want to think of it that way, by the sheer fact that you married me.'

She laughed a little, but not as though she were amused.

'Well, there are the other things. There are the arrangements for Avril to go to Italy——'

'I'm not going to make any bargain with you over that little sweep,' he retorted savagely. 'She can have what she wants. She was prepared to take it anyway, on any terms. It has nothing to do with you.'

'Well, then—Adrian. You can't say Adrian has nothing to do with me. If you support him for the next few years, you must expect something in return.'

'I don't want anything, I tell you.' He was sullen again now, but it was a sort of desperate sullenness.

'You're very—difficult, all at once, Keith. I've set my heart on this thing being done for Adrian.'

'It shall be done,' he said curtly. 'I've given you my word on it.'

'But I will not accept it for nothing.' Ismay's voice was cool and smooth. 'I'm tired of cadging and—what was it? —"paying tomorrow." You can take it that what you did for Father is wiped out by my marrying you, if that's what you want. I'll grant you the best of the argument over Avril. But the day that Adrian goes to medical school—we'll settle accounts. Not the next day or some time in the future. *That day.*'

And without another glance at him she went out of the room, leaving him white and wordless.

CHAPTER EIGHT

Ismay had always supposed—when she thought about it at all—that if married couples had some terrible emotional scene, or row, or whatever you liked to call it, life just refused to go on in the natural channels any longer. Either they separated, or they became like different people, never regaining whatever ground they had in common before.

But she was quite wrong, of course. At least, so far as she herself and Keith were concerned. Perhaps it was because they had never had much ground in common, because they only had to regain a surface politeness, she decided. But, whatever the reason, life was most extraordinarily and unbelievably the same.

Only he never teased her now—never spoke in that half-mocking, laughing way, which she had supposed she hated. In a queer way she missed it, for though a grave, polite Keith at least never ruffled the surface of her composure, somehow she could not help remembering that he had sometimes made her want to laugh against her will, and that he had provoked showers of sparks between them which at least had brilliance, even if they lacked warmth.

For a day or two she refrained from going over to see the family. She was not quite sure why. Either she wanted to give the impression of settling down in her new home, or else she felt that to see them all would raise fresh problems.

When she did decide to go, she meant to say coldly to

Keith something about making arrangements with Adrian now. But, when it came to the point, she lacked the courage even to mention his name, and, instead, she simply said :

'I'm going to see the family this afternoon.'

'Are you? You don't mind if I don't come too, do you? I've got to see about that flooded meadow down by the common.'

'No, I don't mind,' Ismay said. And no one could have imagined from their expressions that to visit the family together would have caused acute embarrassment to both of them.

She walked over in the early afternoon, knowing that Susan would still be at school then and that she would have more opportunity of speaking quietly to Adrian.

The first person she saw, however, was Avril, who was sketching in the garden as usual. Only this time it was on the stretch of rather ragged lawn which lay in front of the house.

She got up at once and came to the gate.

'Hello, Ismay.' Unlike Susan, she did kiss her sister—a cool, sweet kiss that had great charm. 'I wondered when on earth you were coming over. Has married life proved such a success that you can't tear yourself away?'

'Not exactly. I want to talk to you, Avril.' Ismay spoke more curtly than she ever had before to her sister.

'Well, you have a good opportunity.' Avril was completely unconcerned. 'Come and sit here while I go on with this sketch.'

'Where are the others?'

'Adrian's at work——'

'Oh yes, of course.'

'And Father has gone to London.'

'To London!'

'Oh yes. You've no idea how much he enjoys himself, now that money matters have improved. He's a different man.' Avril was in quite a chatty mood.

But Ismay was not. She came straight to the point, now that she knew there was no likelihood of their being interrupted.

'Avril, why did you tell me all those lies about Keith?'

'Which lies?'

'You know what I mean. About your arranging to go away with him—suggesting you had almost started an affair with him. What possessed you to say such things when there was no truth in them at all?'

'I didn't say I had started an affair. In fact, I was particularly careful to point out to you that I had not.'

'But you implied you were on the point of it—that nothing would stop you, if you thought that was the only way of getting to Italy.'

'Well, nothing *would* have stopped me, if that had been the only way.'

'But, Avril, there hadn't been a word said between you! It was all in your imagination—or anticipation—or whatever you like to call it. Yet you spoke as though it had all been arranged. As though he knew at least as much about it as you did.'

'Well (I am sorry it's your husband we're speaking about, Ismay), I don't think I should have had much difficulty in getting him to agree. You see——'

'You most certainly would!' Ismay might be angry with Keith herself, but in this instance she felt he deserved some sort of defence.

'That's a matter of opinion, isn't it?'

'Well, anyway, whatever you thought in the first instance, what possessed you to keep silent when I told you what I had done. I was quite frank with you, Avril. I told you I was marrying him—and why. Yet you never hinted that one part of my reason was based on an entirely false impression. I don't understand you! How could you say nothing—much less *want* to say nothing?'

'I asked you outright if you were doing it specially because of me, and you said "no".'

'Did I?' Poor Ismay was beginning to wonder just what she *had* said in all this tangle.

'You said it was just everything coming together. If you had told me you were doing it simply with some sort of idea of rescuing me, I think I should have explained.'

'You *think* you would?' Ismay passed her hand over her forehead. 'Oh, I'm glad to have that much reassurance,' she added rather bitterly.

Avril glanced at her curiously.

'You didn't do it much for your own sake, did you?'

'For my own sake? No, not at all. How should I?'

'That was a mistake, Ismay. You should always do things partly for your own sake. After all, you're the only person in the world whose wishes you can understand completely, aren't you?'

'Is that how you work things out?' Ismay asked, rather as though she couldn't help it.

Avril nodded.

'I didn't really know how much you wanted this marriage. I only knew that it would be a marvellous thing for me—for all of us—if you did take it on. I should never have urged you, Ismay, but, since you were doing it at all,

I think it was reasonable to suppose that you expected—what shall I say?—some sort of pleasure or profit from it. Well, I didn't see why I should go out of my way to upset all that.'

'You knew I didn't—*couldn't*—care for him at all.'

Avril shrugged.

'All right. But on the other hand, he's an extremely rich man. You may be unworldly, Ismay, but even you can't help knowing that a rich husband is an asset. Besides, he's crazy about you in his way. I suppose that has some attraction. Most girls would jump at a rich and devoted husband, even if they couldn't get up much of a passion for him themselves.'

Ismay didn't answer that, and Avril seemed to think she had explained herself sufficiently, for she went on sketching in silence, while Ismay pulled blades of grass and made a little pile of them.

At last Ismay asked, with irresistible curiosity :

'What did Keith say to you?'

'When?'

'When he came here that evening, and you had to be frank to each other.'

'We didn't need to say very much. I think, perhaps, Ismay, he and I speak the same language—and it's a different language from yours. He's a cynic at heart—just as I am—and——'

'No,' Ismay said absently. 'Not at heart. He's really a romantic by temperament, and a cynic by experience.'

'Think so?' Avril looked amused. 'Well, I dare say you're right. You ought to know. He took it all rather lightly, to tell the truth. Teased me a little and said he was overwhelmed by the rôle I had selected for him. I said

I hoped he would not feel any grudge against me for having assumed so much, and he said——'

'That, on the contrary, he was grateful to you,' finished Ismay, suddenly remembering what she had overheard.

'Something of the sort.'

'I don't know why I don't hate you both,' said Ismay slowly.

'And don't you, Ismay?'

'Well, not you. I can't. You're my sister.'

'He is your husband,' Avril reminded her carelessly. But Ismay made no reply to that, and after a while Avril asked : 'How did you find out about it all? Surely he wasn't so stupid as to tell you himself?'

'No. Susan let it out.'

'She would,' observed Avril without rancour. 'Does he —know?'

'Know what?'

'That you've heard all about it now.'

'Oh yes, of course. He was there at the time. He heard Susan tell me.'

'And couldn't do anything to stop her? How feeble of him.'

Ismay said nothing. She was suddenly very keenly aware of what Keith's feelings must have been as he listened to Susan, blundering innocently through his dreams. But it served him right, of course. No one liked being found out, only, sometimes, some sort of blind justice turned up the truth unexpectedly.

'I suppose,' Avril said coolly, 'there was a row after-wards?'

'I don't think I want to answer that,' Ismay retorted, as she got to her feet. 'I'm going to meet Adrian. I'd like to

154

walk back with him.'

'It's early for him yet,' Avril said, but made no attempt to detain Ismay when she found that she was still determined to go. 'Are you coming back here for tea?'

'Yes, I expect so.'

'That's good,' Avril observed with sincerity. Then she added, 'Things will work out all right, Ismay. I shouldn't worry too much, if I were you.'

'No, I'm sure you wouldn't,' Ismay said dryly, but she smiled a little as she turned away.

For a while after she had left the house, she tried to keep her mind a blank about the things which had been happening. She leant her arms on a gate presently and looked with pleasure at the splashes of colour which a few late poppies made against the yellow corn that was ripe for cutting. She listened to the monotonous chirrup of the grasshoppers in the grass at her feet. And she felt more at peace with the world.

But after a time she remembered that the field at which she was gazing was Keith's field—one of those of which he had spoken with a laugh as 'almost hers', that day she agreed to marry him.

That took a good deal away from her pleasure in it, and brought back her thoughts to the troubles which lay ahead.

Well, anyway, she was going to see Adrian first, which was pleasant. That part at least she was going to enjoy—telling him once and for all that he need not keep on with his hateful, pokey little job, that she and Keith were going to send him to medical school, make him a doctor, and give him his heart's desire.

She was glad he would never know that she had suddenly made *him* the crux of her bargain with Keith. In a way, there was a kind of justice in it, because probably Adrian's eventual work as a doctor would be the only wholly decent thing which would emerge from this horrible tangle.

And Keith *should take his payment* for the things he was doing for them. Never again would she let herself feel under an obligation to the man who had tricked her so completely. Father and his debts might be written off, if he liked. Avril, it was true, made a very doubtful centre for a bargain. But Adrian—— There was something solid about Adrian and his ambitions. Keith should pay for those, according to their arrangement, and, in return, he should accept payment from her. And if his knowledge that she loathed the paying turned his triumph into dust and ashes—well, that was his punishment.

To Ismay, in that moment, it seemed that a harsh sense of justice ran through it all. Keith had schemed unscrupulously to obtain this one thing. Now, in the light of what he had learnt, he knew that to take what he had wanted would be the ruin of his happiness. But he should not be allowed to change his mind now. It was he who had forced the bargain. *Both* sides of it should be carried out. Her pride and, she supposed, some sort of desire for revenge demanded it.

Only—she looked up to see Adrian coming along the road—it was odd to think that Adrian, of all people, should be the instrument of vengeance.

'Hello, Ismay dear !'

As Adrian kissed her, Ismay reflected a little amusedly on the different motives from which the family acted in these matters. Adrian kissed her because he was fond of her. Avril kissed her because she was not. While Susan seldom thought of kissing her at all, because she would have considered it absurd that any sign was necessary to indicate the self-evident fact that of course she was fond of Ismay.

'Have you been home?' Adrian glanced at her affectionately.

'Yes. But I thought I'd walk out and meet you. Then we could come back to tea together.'

'I'm afraid I have to go a good bit out of our way.'

'It doesn't matter. What have you got to do?'

He grinned.

'I'm being a delivery boy. Ours is on holiday, so I've volunteered to take the stuff round myself.'

She laughed, but she was not as amused as he was about it, and presently she burst out :

'Adrian, you won't have to do this any more—this miserable job, I mean. I think you've been wonderful to stick it. But it isn't necessary any longer. Things are quite changed, you see. There isn't the least reason why you shouldn't be a doctor, after all. And you'll be a marvellous doctor, I know. I was only teasing when I spoke about your bedside manner that time. I know your heart's in doctoring, and I can't tell you how happy it makes me to know you can do it, after all.'

She ceased speaking, and there was a short, peculiar silence. Then Adrian said quietly :

'I don't quite understand.'

'Oh, I haven't explained at all properly, of course.' She laughed a little. 'I suppose it's because I'm excited. You see, Keith is willing for me to have anything I like that will—will make the family happy. And what I want more than anything else is that you should have your heart's ambition. I've explained to him, and he's perfectly willing that you should. It's a present from him—from us, Adrian. Isn't it wonderful, really? I think he hardly cares what it costs. You're just to have everything that is necessary. You won't be an assistant to a village chemist any longer. You'll be a doctor—and I shall be frightfully proud of you.'

Again there was a short silence, before Adrian said curiously, 'Are you quite sure you would be proud of me —in those circumstances?'

'Why—why, of course.' She almost stammered in her astonishment. 'What is wrong, Adrian?'

'Nothing. Except that I couldn't possibly accept. I shouldn't dream of it for one moment.'

'But I don't understand. I *want* you to have it. Keith wants you to have it. What is there against it?'

He didn't answer her at once, but, taking her by the arm, he fell into step beside her.

'Ismay, you didn't marry Keith Otterbury because you were in love with him at all, did you?'

Ismay was dumb.

'No, I thought not. You married him because we were in a hell of a mess, and you didn't see how we could get out of it without someone's money to help us. I don't know which of us you had most in mind. I thought at the time that it was Father, and that was why I couldn't say much. If you couldn't face seeing him bankrupt and broken, and you were willing to make some sort of sacrifice to prevent it, that was your affair. I think perhaps I should have done the same if I had had the chance. But for me to take Otterbury's money would be a very differ-

ent matter. I couldn't, Ismay dear. It would be a betrayal
—not only of you, but of everything that mattered in our
family relations.'

'But I want to do this for you,' Ismay whispered.

'I know you do. But do you know, darling, that that
isn't even very important?'

'To you, you mean?'

'No, I didn't mean that. Of course it's important to me
that you think so much about my happiness. But it isn't
just a question of your wanting to do this thing for me or
my wanting to have it done. We don't often talk about
things like love and respect, Ismay. Ordinary families
don't—it makes one uncomfortable to do it often. But of
course, there *is* such a thing, and it's pretty important.
Suppose you heard in theory of a brother who let his sister
marry a rich man whom she didn't want, and then built
his career on the proceeds. You wouldn't think much of
him, would you? It isn't any different because you are the
sister and I the brother. If I let you—or rather, Keith—
finance me now, it would mean that something very
important went out of our relationship. Can't you see
that?'

She was silent—actually trembling a little—because
everything which Adrian was saying was more or less what
she had tried to explain to Keith that other evening. Only
she wanted Adrian to have his ambition and his happiness.
She wanted something—something decent and worthwhile to happen out of her bargain with Keith. She didn't
want it all to be for nothing.

'But what will you do, Adrian? Don't you hate this life
of yours? How can you possibly turn your back on the
chance to do exactly what you always wanted?' She

couldn't accept his answer without trying once more to persuade him. But she knew quite well, even as she advanced the arguments, that they were not going to have any weight.

Adrian shrugged his shoulders.

'What shall I do? Study for all I'm worth. I ought to have begun long ago, but it's not too late. For a start, I shall try for my "A" levels next summer. Astley thinks I shall get them, too.'

'Oh, Adrian!'

'What?'

'It seems so small after all your hopes.'

'I know. But it's something that I can tackle with my own resources and ability. I've finished with building castles in the air on expectations of what other people will do for me. Just lately I've begun to wonder why the hell I thought I *should* have opportunities handed to me. I'll just have to make them, like other people. I can't say when they will come, but I'm jolly well not going to wait for them to happen. There's been a great deal too much of that in our family—and where has it got us?'

Ismay was silent. And after a while, looking at her troubled face, Adrian said :

'What is it, Ismay?'

'Nothing. I know you're quite right, but I wish you were wrong. I'd got it all worked out so beautifully for you.'

He laughed and took her arm again.

'You can't live other people's lives for them, Ismay, however much you want to move all the difficulties out of their paths. I'm sorry to sound so much the ancient philosopher this afternoon, but I've been thinking a good deal since Great-aunt Georgina dealt us that nasty crack from

the grave, so to speak. Maybe she did us a service, after all
—though she'd just hate to think so.'

Ismay smiled slightly. She liked to hear this new note
of optimism and self-reliance in Adrian's voice, but her
plans certainly had gone badly awry.

'So there really isn't any more to say about it?' she said
at last.

'No, there just isn't any more to say, except—thank you
for wanting to do it, Ismay. Did I say that?'

She felt it hardly mattered whether he had said it or
not.

As they turned back in the direction of home, Adrian
seemed to think it was his turn to ask a few questions,
because he said—just a little too carelessly, perhaps :

'How are things turning out with you, Ismay? Is Keith
proving the answer to a maiden's prayer?'

'He's very good and generous,' Ismay assured him
hastily. Whereat Adrian laughed.

' "Good," eh? First time anyone's handed that to Keith
Otterbury, I should think.'

Ismay was faintly embarrassed, hardly knowing what to
say. She and Adrian had always had so much in common
that it was very difficult to tell him anything but the exact
truth. And yet the true state of affairs between her and
Keith would hardly bear telling, quite apart from the fact
that one *had* a sense of loyalty towards one's husband—
even such a problematical husband as Keith.

'You don't need to worry about me, Adrian. Everything
is working out—working out marvellously.'

'I'm glad to hear it,' Adrian said. But she knew from
his expression that he meant, 'Well, I suppose it is your
private affair, but don't expect me to believe *that* one.'

When they reached home, not only Susan, but Father too had returned, and he greeted Ismay with dignified affection.

'Dear child, let me look at you'—rather as though she might have changed beyond recognition in the interval—'very charming. The married state suits you, I see. Well, my dear, there is nothing more dignifying—more ennobling—than a happy marriage, as I have always said.' He never had said so before, because it had never happened to be appropriate to the occasion, but no one recalled that—least of all Father.

Ismay smiled and assured him that she was indeed very happy, and, somewhat to her surprise, Susan added suddenly :

'Yes, I know. I've seen her and Keith together in their own home, and they're *both* happy.'

This having been satisfactorily established, Father turned to his own affairs. Ismay saw at once that Avril had said nothing less than the truth. Father was indeed a changed man, now that he was free from financial embarrassment. Ismay doubted if he even remembered now that someone else had had to pay his debts for him. They were paid—that was all that mattered. And now he was free to indulge in characteristic little expenses once more, from his small but unencumbered income.

Oh yes, life was very good to Father just now. He even remarked, with a pleasantly reflective air :

'I think, Avril my dear, that when you go to take up your studies in Florence, I shall be tempted to come with you for a while. Ah, how many years since I saw Italy? Indeed the land of sunshine and laughter.'

'Also mosquitoes,' Adrian reminded him, because they all felt it was extremely unlikely that Avril would want his company.

But there they were wrong. Avril stared thoughtfully at Father and remarked:

'Do you know, I think that's rather a good idea. I could be lots freer to do anything I wanted if I were obviously in the care of a distinguished and very British-looking parent.'

Father liked the 'distinguished' but was not quite so sure that the 'very British' gave exactly the impression he wished to create.

'That is rather a curious way of putting it, Avril,' he said, smilingly firm. 'Heaven knows, no man is prouder than I of being an Englishman. But I think you will find that abroad I shall be taken for something of a cosmopolitan.'

It was difficult to see how Father, who had passed almost the whole of his life in one spot, could have become cosmopolitan, but no one grudged him his little indulgence. And even Avril said absently, 'I dare say,' because she was very intent on working out this new idea to her own advantage.

'And what'd *we* do?' Susan was rather indignant about these plans which so obviously excluded herself.

'You and Adrian?' Avril remembered them with difficulty. 'Oh, you can look after yourselves for once. Besides, Ismay would be close at hand to run over and see you got on all right. Father, I think it's a marvellous idea. You won't have a penny to pay for my expenses'—she didn't even glance at Ismay as she said that—'so you could manage very well, couldn't you?'

'It would take some thinking over.' Father showed faint signs of caution, now that he realised Avril was rushing him. But it was obvious to all of them that he was already enjoying in anticipation the rôle of 'distinguished parent' to the very pretty and charming art student that his daughter would make.

'Well, of course,' Avril conceded. 'But don't let's think it over too long, because we want to be nicely settled there before the winter. Oh, are you going, Ismay?'

'Yes.' Ismay had got up. 'I think Keith will expect me back by now.'

'My goodness,' Susan observed, 'you are a nice obedient wife, aren't you? Doesn't he let you out for long at a time?'

'Of course, you little goose,' Ismay laughed. But she refused their pressing invitations to stay any longer.

She was glad too that no one offered to accompany her part of the way back to Otterbury Hall. She very much wanted to be alone, and think over the events of the afternoon. Or rather, of course, they were not exactly events. They were odd side issues to the general problem of herself and Keith.

Somehow, the sight of Father—dear but shameless old spendthrift that he was—and Avril, enthusiastically arranging their Italian trip on the strength of Keith's money made her feel ashamed. If it had been Adrian, and his much more worthwhile plans, it would not have mattered so much.

But Adrian had chosen to reject the offer she and Keith had made to him. Even now, she could hardly believe that, and the sharpness of disappointment seemed even keener.

She was tired, she discovered, and her head ached. Or perhaps it was just her heart. But anyway, the way back to Otterbury Hall seemed very long indeed—even across the fields that were 'almost hers'.

When she reached home, one of the servants informed her that Mr. Otterbury was out in the garden, and, irresistibly, she felt drawn to go out and talk to him.

She found him by the gate that led from the garden into the orchard, and he was talking to one of the outdoor staff as she came up. For a moment he didn't notice her standing there. Then the man murmured something and drew Keith's attention to her.

'Why, Ismay!' He turned to her at once. 'I didn't see you. Have you been home long?'

'No. I—came straight out here.'

He glanced at her curiously but made no comment on that, and they began to stroll slowly back towards the house.

'Are they all well at home?'

'Oh yes, thank you. Father is particularly on top of the world.'

He didn't ask why. Perhaps he guessed that without inquiring. There was a slight pause. Then in a tone that was elaborately casual, he said :

'Did you see Adrian?'

'Oh yes.'

'And had you any chance of a discussion with him?'

'Yes.'

She thought she heard him draw a deep breath, but his voice was still cool as he asked :

'And what did you arrange?'

'Nothing.'

'Nothing!'

'No. He just—refused.' And suddenly she began to cry very forlornly.

CHAPTER NINE

THERE was a strange little silence. Then Keith said softly, and with quite extraordinary sincerity:

'Thank God!'

Somehow she was even more acutely aware of that than of the fact that he had put his arm round her and was leading her away from the house again. Presently he made her sit down on a seat that was screened from any inquisitive eyes by masses of rambler roses that grew over it.

He sat beside her, his arm still round her, but he made no attempt to check her crying, and after a moment she stopped of her own accord, with an apologetic murmur about 'being sorry she was such an idiot'.

'You have no reason to apologise for anything,' he told her, and there was a slight emphasis on the pronoun. 'Will you tell me just what happened?'

'There—there isn't really much to tell. I explained to him that you—that we wanted him to carry out his ambition to become a doctor, and that you were willing to support him through his training. He—refused to accept it. Quite nicely—but he refused.'

'Why, Ismay? Did he tell you that?'

'Yes. He said—that he knew I had married you because of the money—I'm sorry, Keith——'

'You need not be. Go on.'

'And he said that if I wanted to do that for Father's sake it was my own affair, but that if *he* took any of your money it would be an entirely different matter. He—he thought it would be a sort of betrayal of our family feeling.'

'He said just that?'

'Yes.'

'Then you have no reason to cry, Ismay.' He smiled very slightly, though she noticed that his eyes remained grave and even a little heavy. 'It seems that Adrian felt exactly as you did about loyalty inside your family circle. Do you remember—you thought all that had been spoilt?'

'Yes, I remember,' she said slowly.

'Well, so far as Adrian was concerned, the family ties or unity or whatever you like to call it stood the strain. You're a little disappointed because you can't make Adrian a great doctor, but aren't you damned glad that he had enough character to refuse to sponge on you?'

She was silent, in something between pleasure and astonishment at the discovery of the truth of this. And after a moment he said reflectively :

'So the casual Adrian was the one who withstood temptation. Queer—I shouldn't have given him credit for so much character.'

'Adrian! He has ten times as much character as anyone like *you* !' Ismay flared to the defence of her brother.

'Humbling, but true,' Keith agreed, and for the first time for some while she saw the old mocking amusement light up his eyes. That 'Thank God' of his had been no figure of speech. He was fervently, passionately glad that Adrian had refused his offer.

'This leaves us in a rather—odd position, doesn't it?' She said that without looking at him.

'I don't see that.' A touch of stubbornness crept into his voice. 'I think it has smoothed out several difficulties, and it has certainly left me very thankful to find that I haven't caused quite such a flutter in the Laverhope dovecot after all.'

She looked at him then, those blue eyes of hers dark and rather wide open with the directness of her glance.

'Have you forgotten that we made Adrian a sort of— test case?'

'No, I haven't forgotten. And for that reason I'm even more thankful that he refused our offer,' he said curtly.

An innocent air of reflection, more suited to Avril than to Ismay, came into her eyes then.

'For a man who drives a hard bargain,' she said slowly, 'you're strangely anxious not to have me pay up, aren't you?'

'And for a woman who married me reluctantly, you're strangely anxious to throw yourself at my head,' he retorted brutally, as he got to his feet.

'Keith!' She was so astounded that she could hardly even utter his name. Whatever she had expected, it was not that. One of his violent, half-sullen protestations that he loved her, perhaps—or even a difficult, reluctant admission that his high-handed ways had ruined his own happiness as well as hers. But this—insult!

'I don't think I quite understand you,' she said softly and coldly, the strangest feeling of dismayed anger creeping round her heart as she spoke.

'You don't? Well, perhaps that's just as well,' he told her lightly, 'because I have a horrible suspicion that I was speaking at that moment like the "outsider" I am.'

He smiled straight at her—casually, carelessly, almost insolently, quite in his old manner.

'All the same it would be interesting to know what you

did mean.' She found suddenly that, if he could be cool and casual, so could she. 'By your charming description of me as "throwing myself at your head" are you implying that I'm showing an unwelcome fondness?'

'We-ell, not fondness, exactly.' His eyes danced impertinently. 'Shall we say—an embarrassing conscientiousness in your desire to carry out all your wifely duties?'

'How—*dare* you!' She sprang to her feet in her turn. 'What, in heaven's name, *do* you want of me? You come thrusting your way into my bedroom, demanding your rights in the most revolting manner——'

'Not demanding, my dear,' he pointed out smoothly.

'You practically call me a cheat to my face,' she rushed on furiously, not heeding his interruption. 'Then when I bring myself to—to play fair, or whatever you like to call it, you say I'm throwing myself at your head. I don't understand you and your disgusting, cynical ways!'

'No? But do you understand, my little Ismay, that there's such a thing as giving a man enough time to discover he's made a mistake?'

'Made—a mistake?' she repeated, stupefied.

'Exactly.'

'You mean—you don't—love me, after all?' It was queer to use such expressions to him.

'You're forcing me to be dreadfully ungallant.'

'I don't care about gallantry or the lack of it. Please tell me the truth.'

'Well then, the truth is that two years of romantic imaginings are one thing. Two weeks of practical experience are something else. I think you yourself told me I was a fool to think I could build an undying passion on nothing. You were right, of course. It's humiliating to find that a cynic like myself could be a romantic fool, but there it is. I suppose a good many better men than I have made the same mistake.'

'You mean,' Ismay said levelly, 'that so long as I was out of reach, I was eminently desirable. As soon as you had married me, you lost interest in me.'

'My dear girl'—he made a slight grimace—'Susan herself could hardly have put it in more unpalatable form.'

'I dare say not. But I'm not in a mood to wrap things up prettily. And while home truths are being handed round, you may as well know that I think you the most unutterable swine I've ever met!'

'No doubt you're right,' he agreed regretfully. 'I imagine a Laverhope's experience of swine is strictly limited.'

But Ismay hardly heard his reply, for she had turned on her heel and was now walking rapidly towards the house.

He made no attempt to follow her, and she gained the safety of her own room without meeting any of the servants.

For the first few moments, she was too angry and agitated even to sit down and think. She walked up and down her room, her eyes bright, her cheeks hot with indignation and anger. Not that she cared in the least, of course, about losing his remarkably worthless affection. But the casual cynicism of it all revolted her.

To think that he should marry her—indeed, any girl—for a whim, and then calmly admit that he didn't want her after all! It made one wonder just how many of the other disreputable stories about him were true. And it made one sick with dismay to realise that *this was one's husband.*

Not that he was her husband in any real sense—or that he was ever likely to be. That, at least, was something for which to be thankful. But what did one *do*? How did one go on with life after anything like the last few shattering weeks?

Ismay sat down on the side of her bed at last—tired suddenly, and utterly dispirited. She felt that not only had her roots been torn up out of familiar ground, but the new ground which offered was too unspeakably shallow for one to take root again. She was used to doing things for deep and genuine reasons, not to be tossed hither and thither for the sake of some casual impulse that was gone almost before it was formed.

She had not taken her marriage lightly. She had only been dismayed by its peculiar circumstances, anxious to have time in which to adapt herself to a set of circumstances that were entirely strange to her.

Now—before she could do any adapting, the whole thing was swept away again. She was married, and she was not married. She had created a rather frightening passion in her husband, and she had made him indifferent. She owed him a great deal and he was amused and bored that she wanted to pay up honestly.

There was no sense in it anywhere. And there was no dignity or kindly feeling or humour or any of the things that made life worth living.

For a few seconds Ismay was very near tears again. Then she reminded herself that she had already cried an absurd amount that evening. 'And I refuse to cry because of anything that *he* does or says,' she told herself bitterly.

Somehow life had to go on, of course. She was not quite sure how. But at least he should not have the satisfaction of supposing she was making herself unhappy about anything he did.

Rather slowly Ismay began to change for dinner.

As she did so, her thoughts grew quieter and her judgment cooler. She remembered that he had been genuinely relieved that Adrian had shown up so well. He had even said something about being glad that he had caused less harm than he had first thought in the Laverhope family. She supposed that was something to his credit, though, of course, it might be nothing more than a casually good-natured desire to see no ill-effects from his own behaviour.

She wondered if he had some idea now of cutting his losses—somehow getting rid of the young wife he found he no longer wanted. It was possible—and anyway, Ismay suddenly decided, she was not going to remain in a state of uncertainty and indecision. She would have it out with him. He should not imagine that she was waiting breathlessly for his decision.

At dinner it was difficult to find an opportunity. But, afterwards, when they were having coffee together in the lounge, while the french windows stood open to the warm, scented evening, she spoke abruptly.

'Keith, I want to talk to you.'

'Yes?' He glanced across at her lazily and smiled. 'I know. It's about Avril, isn't it?'

'About Avril? Certainly not! There's nothing more to say about Avril. At least—what made you say that?'

'Only that she telephoned just before dinner. I understand she's anxious to start on her Italian trip as soon as possible. I also gather that your father is going with her. She wanted to know what I thought of the arrangement.'

'About Father going?' Ismay's voice sharpened slightly in spite of herself.

'Yes.'

'I don't see what that part of the arrangement has to do with you,' she said quickly.

'Don't you?' The air of ironical amusement deepened.

'Keith? You don't mean that she suggested you should —you should——'

'Pay? Well, I'm afraid she did, Ismay.'

'Oh, they're incorrigible—Avril and Father!' Ismay spoke her thoughts aloud in her annoyance and distress. 'I suppose—I hope—you refused very sharply.'

'No, I agreed.'

'But *why*? It's unnecessary for you to pander to Father like that. He's had his debts paid. He's relieved from real financial worry. There was no need to indulge him in this. Why should you pay any more, Keith?'

'You can call it conscience money, if you like,' he grinned at her.

'Please don't be absurd.'

'But it's true.' It was hard to say whether that quick return to gravity was genuine or mocking. 'My conscience —such as it is—has given me some uncomfortable jars over the part I've played in your family affairs.'

'You've been very generous to us,' Ismay said coldly.

'Not to you.' He said that softly, and with a peculiar intonation she could not quite understand.

'Well, anyway'—she was a trifle agitated now, though she could not have said why—'there's no reason for you to pay out still more money for us.'

'Your father is very anxious to go, Ismay.'

'Yes, I know. But he always is anxious to do anything that will amuse him and cost money. If he wants it so much, let him pay for himself. I know that sounds hard. But though Father is a darling, he's an absolutely graceless old spendthrift. It's hardly even his own fault. Everyone always encouraged him to be just that. It isn't necessary for you to do this thing, Keith. It—it's all wrong in principle, too.'

Keith didn't laugh at her that time. He got up from his chair, thrusting his hands into his pockets in that characteristic manner, and walking slowly up the room and back again, as he had that first evening she had come here. Then he paused beside her and, looking down at her, said rather deliberately :

'Don't you think it might be very convenient for you and me if your father, as well as Avril, were out of the district during the next few months?'

'Convenient?' Ismay looked up at him in surprise. 'How do you mean?'

'My dear, so far as one can undo a mistake, you and I are going to have to undo this mistaken marriage of ours. I don't know that it's going to be specially easy if we have to explain every step to your—somewhat conventional parent. If he and Avril are in Italy, there will be only Adrian and Susan to consider. Adrian will be busy with his work, and in any case, he more than half understands the situation already, while even Susan must surely give some part of her attention to her school work. She won't have so very much to spare for what we're doing.'

'And what,' asked Ismay, with slightly dry lips, 'shall we be doing?'

He gave her a quick glance at that, perhaps because of the tone of her voice.

'The usual way of undoing a marriage is to arrange a divorce,' he said curtly.

She was silent, and after a moment, he added :

'I suppose you have no objection to that, have you?'

Even then she hardly knew what she wanted to say. No doubt this was the best—indeed, the only—solution. But how futile—how sordid the whole business was! It might be quite an ordinary occurrence in his sort of life, but it was a hateful and incongruous thing to happen to Ismay Laverhope.

'You're quite used to this sort of thing, aren't you?' she said, unaware that she had not answered his question, and putting her own inquiry rather as though she could not help it.

His eyebrows shot up.

'I haven't figured in a divorce suit before, if that's what you mean.'

'No, I didn't mean quite that. But it—it's nothing to you to indulge in some extravagant fancy for ages, feed it with your own romantic ideas, force some preposterous issue for the sake of it, and then suddenly abandon the whole thing by way of the divorce court.'

She thought she must have made him very angry by her candour, because his voice was slightly harsh as he said :

'You didn't answer my question, you know. Have you any objection to a divorce?'

'No. I suppose it—it's the only way out.'

'I don't see any other. We'll keep up some sort of appearances until your father and Avril have gone abroad. Then I expect it will be pleasanter for you if I go to London for a while. We can arrange the rest through my solicitors.'

She didn't answer that. Perhaps there was nothing to answer. But she suddenly felt unutterably sad and overwhelmed by a sense of failure. It was a terrible thing to have taken on such a solemn business as marriage—even so strange a marriage as theirs had been—and then abandon it like that, with hardly an attempt to make anything of it.

For a moment she was sorely tempted to take his hand, make some little gesture of intimacy and friendship, and ask him if he didn't think they ought to make a better trial of things than this. But she remembered just in time how he had mockingly accused her of 'throwing herself at his head'. There really was nothing else to do about it—nothing she could say or even hint.

They had made a rotten tangle of things—the sort of tangle one could not undo. The only way was to cut it.

Those next few days were not happy days for Ismay. It was impossible to ignore someone who was living in the same house. And yet it was impossible to decide what attitude to take. He was very polite to her in his careless, smiling way, but somehow that made things no easier.

'I know what it is,' thought Ismay unhappily. 'I hate living on the surface of things. We never did that at home. Susan would have prevented it if no one else had,' she reflected with a faint smile. It was strange, too, to feel that there was no one who either needed her or wanted her.

She went over to see the family several times, but everyone seemed frantically engaged in the task of dispatching Father and Avril on their journey, and no one had very much time for anything else.

'My goodness, I don't know what all the hurry is about,' Susan confided to her. 'You'd think, after they'd waited all this time to make up their minds, they could bear to waste a day or two instead of rushing around like hens in a hen-coop.'

Ismay hoped she had not presented this comparison for Father's inspection.

'One always does things in a hurry in the end, I suppose,' she said tolerantly. 'At least, the Laverhopes always do.'

'Yes. Like your marriage,' Susan agreed. 'But then that was romantic.'

Ismay thought not, but refrained from saying anything.

Of Avril—when she was helping her to pack—she did inquire :

'Was it your idea or Father's that Keith should pay for you both?'

Avril looked up absently from what she was doing, and Ismay repeated her question a little more sharply.

'Oh—both, I think. We sort of worked it out together. Father had been dipping pretty well into his own income again, you know, and of course this sort of trip is rather a luxury from his point of view.'

'You weren't at all ashamed about it?'

Avril looked faintly surprised.

'About what, Ismay?'

'About asking Keith for even more than he had spilt on the family already.'

'We-ell'—Avril smiled winningly, and for a moment she looked curiously like Father—'it isn't much good having a terribly rich brother-in-law if you don't make use of him. Besides, I think he almost likes doing it. He's so crazy about you that he gets a real kick out of making extravagant gestures where the family are concerned.'

Ismay wondered what Avril would have done if she had coolly retorted, 'Keith is already tired of me.'

Instead, she said :

'What makes you think he's so crazy about me?'

Again Avril gave her that look of faint surprise.

'Why, everything, of course. The way he looks at you, the things he does for you—even the way he engineered your marriage. And he's extravagant about his affections, just as he is about everything else. It's embarrassing, I should think, but very useful,' Avril concluded cryptically.

Ismay felt tempted to point out that extravagances, of necessity, never lasted long, and that this one had already died a natural death. But she was silent, and, after a moment, Avril added, with an air of impersonal reflection :

'Keith is the kind of man to be extravagant even in his sacrifices. Do you think I could wear that red belt with my grey frock, or will it make my hair look pink?'

'Nothing on earth,' Ismay assured her, 'would make your hair look pink. Red-gold it is, and red-gold it will remain, whatever you wear.'

'I dare say you're right.'

'And I don't think Keith is given to sacrificing himself —extravagantly or otherwise,' Ismay added crisply.

'Think not? Well, I expect you know your own husband best,' Avril conceded equably. 'But I imagine he was the kind of child who planned dramatic rescues in which he got killed, saving whoever he adored at the moment.'

She dismissed the subject of Keith after that, in favour

of the much more interesting one of her outfit. But her words lingered most strangely in Ismay's mind.

Queer that Avril should have said just that. It reminded her very sharply of Keith describing himself and his mother.

'I imagined all sorts of dramatic scenes in which I rescued her from wild bulls and other improbable animals——'

She had felt sorry for him at that moment, she remembered. There had been a queer chord of sympathy struck between them. She had even kissed him—lightly, but of her own accord—the only time she had kissed him voluntarily.

That had been a very different Keith from the uncaring man with whom she now lived. Or rather—Ismay corrected herself grimly—in whose house she now lived.

'I wish I hadn't—lost that.'

She had no idea she had spoken aloud until Avril said :
'Um? What have you lost?'

'Nothing.' Ismay roused herself. 'Nothing that matters.'

But she knew suddenly that it was something which mattered very much indeed. The connecting link between herself and the generous, extravagant, warm-hearted creature that her husband could be.

The preparations for departure culminated in a grand finale in which the whole family—including even Keith— escorted the two travellers to the station.

'Mind you write pretty often,' Susan said. 'It'll help my stamp collection enormously having some of the family living abroad.'

'I hope, my dear, that will not be your only reason for

wishing to hear from us.' Father spoke, with genial reproach.

'Oh no,' Susan assured him generously. 'We shall want to hear all about your adventures. People who go abroad always have adventures.'

'Ah, *Dio mio*, but only when one is young,' exclaimed Father, with humorous regret. (He would never have dreamed of using the expression 'My God' to any of his children, but these things sounded different in a foreign tongue. In any case, the small book in his pocket, which bade him 'brush up his Italian' authorised the expression quite frequently.)

'Well, Avril can have the adventures and you can write home about them,' Susan said. But Father evidently considered this an unsuitable division of labour, because he said very firmly :

'We'll see, childie, we'll see.'

Ismay wondered if anyone would thank Keith, as the person almost wholly responsible for this trip abroad. Not with any crude references to paying bills, of course, but gracefully and with some real heart about it.

No one did, however, and she thought suddenly that it was no wonder he regarded them all with cynical amusement. On impulse she turned away with him from the group, as though she wanted to draw his attention to something at the other end of the platform.

'I suppose you're thinking we're a pretty dreadful crowd, aren't you?' she said abruptly.

'Ismay !—no.' He looked genuinely surprised. 'Rather dear and amusing.'

'Funny—that's how I used to see us,' she said slowly.

'You'll see them like that again,' he told her quite gently. But before she could ask him what he meant by that, Susan piped excitedly :

'Here comes the train !'

Even then, Father took leisurely and dignified farewell of his family. It took more than an irate porter, crying 'Hurry along there, please,' to disturb Father in the middle of a set speech.

The united efforts of the family, however, got him into the railway carriage, and if the best and final passages were declaimed as the train drew out of the station, no one really minded. As Susan said, it was 'rather effective to hear it dying away in the distance.'

CHAPTER TEN

As they came out of the station, Ismay said :

'You two had better come back with us to the Hall for tea.'

'Thanks, but I have to get back to the shop,' Adrian said. Never once, she noticed, had he come to Otterbury Hall since she had married Keith.

'And I *promised* to go to tea with Carol,' Susan assured her regretfully. 'She thought it would cheer me up.'

Ismay thought Susan looked singularly little in need of cheering, but she accepted the excuses with a smile, and, after brief good-byes, the group broke up, Ismay and Keith driving back home alone.

In the car it was he who spoke first, and then only to observe conventionally :

'I expect you'll miss them a good deal, Ismay.'

'Yes. But not so much as if I had still been at home.'

At the mention of that, he gave her a quick glance. Then after a moment he said, with rather elaborate casualness :

'Shall you go home again—later ?'

'After the divorce, you mean ?' She got that out with difficulty.

'Yes, after the divorce.'

'I—don't know. I suppose so—yes. There won't be anywhere else to go.'

'You could travel.' His voice sounded abrupt, even

slightly harsh, against the soft, purring background of the motor.

'Alone? I don't think I should like that,' Ismay said slowly, and conversation languished.

As he drew the car to a standstill outside the house, he said :

'I want to talk to you, Ismay. Will you come into the garden?'

She got out of the car without a word, and, as though by common consent, they strolled past the house and towards the seat where they had sat that evening they discussed Adrian's refusal.

The late afternoon light was still warm and clear, and there was something almost languid in the heavy-scented quiet which lay over the garden.

But there was nothing languid in the attitude of either Keith or Ismay. She felt tense and strung up, and, glancing at the peculiar set of his mouth, she thought he felt the same.

Even when they were sitting down, he seemed to find some difficulty in framing what he wanted to say, and presently she asked :

'What is it, Keith?'

'Oh'—he made one of his characteristic little gestures of impatience—'there are a lot of practical details you and I have to settle. We must talk them over, only it's difficult to begin. It all sounds so—crude.'

'But then most things about this business have been crude, haven't they, Keith?' She said without rancour— even a little sadly, and she saw him unexpectedly bite his lip.

'Crude. It's a soul-destroying word, isn't it?' he said

sombrely, and, as though he hardly noticed what he was doing, he took her hand in his, and gazed at the ring which he had bought in Athens because it was the colour of her eyes.

She was silent, not knowing what to say to him, and after a moment he put her hand quickly away from him, as though realising suddenly what he was doing.

'It's about this—divorce.' There could hardly, thought Ismay, have been anything more crude than the way he introduced that. 'I'll see to everything, of course—but I'm afraid it's bound to be a difficult time for you until everything is settled. I'm sorry—I would have had it otherwise if I could. But perhaps, in the queer little way you have of working things out to yourself, you'll allow yourself to feel that washes out any—any obligation you feel towards me.'

She smiled faintly.

'That doesn't sound very logical, Keith, but I think I know what you mean. Only please don't think anything I've done or—or had to put up with really does cancel out your generosity——'

He moved sharply, but she put her hand lightly on his arm to prevent any interruption.

'No, listen to me, please. I'm very conscious of the fact that we have been ungrateful—that *I* have been ungrateful. I know there have been hard words between us, and I know you have done some not very admirable things. But you have been fantastically generous in other ways——'

'With money, you mean?'

'Very well, with money. But that happened to be what we needed.'

'It's easy to be generous about money when you're rich,' he told her a trifle gloomily.

Ismay laughed with genuine amusement.

'Great-aunt Georgina didn't think so. But anyway, that doesn't really matter. You *were* generous, while I——'

'Ismay—please!'

'No, I'm not going to say any more about "paying up" or "cancelling things out". It was rather silly ever to talk in that vein anyway. But do you know, I don't think I ever even thanked you.'

'Child, I don't want your thanks.' He gave a rather unhappy little laugh, and those bright, insolent eyes of his fell, as they had once or twice before when she had seriously put him out.

'No, I dare say not. But I'd like to say it, all the same. Thank you, Keith.'

'You make me feel a hound.'

She laughed again, and once more it was with genuine amusement.

'I expect a man always feels frightfully uncomfortable with a woman he has grown tired of,' she said equably.

There was a queer silence. Then he said rather flatly: 'I expect so.'

'Well'—she hesitated—'was that all there was to say?'

'Yes. Except that—I'm sorry I made such a hash of things for you. It was as you said once—thrusting my way in because I was a little jealous of something I didn't understand. I hope I haven't spoilt everything for you, Ismay. I hope when all this is over, you'll go back to the kind of life you like, and be happy again.'

She knew suddenly that one never went back—that it was no good thinking things would ever be the same again. But there was no point in telling him that now.

'You won't have to—worry about anything, you know.

There'll always be plenty of—money for you.'

'But'—Ismay sprang to her feet suddenly—'if we separate like this——' She stopped suddenly, for when she sprang up she realised, from the momentary tug on her dress, that he had been holding a fold of skirt in that agitated, almost childlike way he had once before when he was trying to explain something to her.

She stared down at his dark bent head—at the curious little network of crumples in her frock. He must have been holding her desperately tightly to make such clear marks, she thought irrelevantly. Something, like a warning little bell at the back of her mind, told her that she ought to be able to read some significance into those crumples—that the hold which he had relaxed immediately had been desperately tight because he was—desperate.

And then suddenly casual, careless, impersonal words of Avril's drifted back into her mind, 'Keith is the kind of man to be extravagant even in his sacrifices.'

The most extraordinary emotions rose like a tide in Ismay's heart—astonishment, pity, amusement and the strangest tenderness. No wonder she hardly knew whether she wanted to laugh or cry. She glanced down at him again. He was perfectly still—curiously still, as though he were a little afraid of something.

'Keith,' she said softly, and he moved then, 'I'm going to say something—something rather outrageous to you. No, please don't look at me, because, if I had any proper pride, I shouldn't be saying this at all.'

'Well?' He looked away across the garden, and she saw that he looked curiously pale and bleak.

'If I—begged you to give up this idea of a divorce—told you that I—I want most terribly to give our married

187

life a chance, what would you say?'

Without a word, he turned and put his arms round her waist, burying his head against her and holding her more tightly than anyone had ever held her before.

'Ismay, Ismay, Ismay.'

She would never have believed that the repetition of her name could have hurt so much.

'Don't, darling.' She bent over him eagerly, the unfamiliar endearment springing quite naturally to her lips. 'It's all right—I'm not going away. I mean—I'm not going to let you go away.'

'I love you so much,' he whispered almost incoherently. 'It's all so hopeless—everything I did was wrong—so crude when I wanted it to be beautiful—so sordid when I wanted to be generous. I don't understand you—I only love you. But I could do nothing but ruin your life. That's why I thought the only thing was to wash it all out—to pretend you didn't even matter any more. Then you wouldn't be uncomfortable and remorseful about me. I could just get out again and leave you alone.'

'But I don't want you to leave me alone.'

His arms tightened again convulsively, and she knew that no one had ever loved and needed her as this man did. The family—yes, in their way, but never with the fierce and desperate intensity of her husband.

She sat down slowly, drawing him quite naturally against her.

'Are we starting all over again?' she whispered.

'I don't know, love. It's just exactly as you say.' He spoke in a whisper too.

'Aren't you ever going to look up at me again?'

'Oh——' he looked up then with a shamefaced little

laugh. 'Oh, lord, I'm sorry! I've crumpled your dress terribly—and made a fool of myself into the bargain.'

'I don't think you're a fool at all,' Ismay said slowly, 'except for letting a raffish set of scroungers like the Laverhopes impose upon you.'

'Ismay! You shan't call yourselves that.'

'Oh, don't worry. None of the others would—and I only should in certain moods.'

'Darling—you're laughing a little?'

'Yes, of course. I always laugh about the family. Mother used to say it was the only way of living with us and not going mad.'

'Do you know that you had stopped laughing about them in the last few weeks? You'd begun to take them seriously.' He was smiling at her now himself, and she realised then how much strain had gone from his expression.

'Keith, that must have been what was the matter. I took them seriously and that made me go a little mad. That was why I didn't realise——'

'Didn't realise what, darling?'

'That—I was falling in love with you.'

'Ismay'—he took her very gently in his arms—'you're not laughing at *me* now, are you?' and there was real anxiety in his eyes.

'No.' She kissed him smilingly. 'Not just at the moment. But you must let me laugh at you a little sometimes. One always laughs a little about the people one loves best.'

28 best sellers

Here are 28 re-issues from the Harlequin
Romance Library specially reprinted
because of demand.

- [ ] 901 HOPE FOR TOMORROW
  Anne Weale
- [ ] 902 MOUNTAIN OF DREAMS
  Barbara Rowan
- [ ] 903 SO LOVED AND SO FAR
  Elizabeth Hoy
- [ ] 904 MOON AT THE FULL
  Susan Barrie
- [ ] 909 DESERT DOORWAY
  Pamela Kent
- [ ] 911 RETURN OF SIMON
  Celine Conway
- [ ] 912 THE DREAM AND THE
  DANCER   Eleanor Farnes
- [ ] 919 DEAR INTRUDER
  Jane Arbor
- [ ] 928 THE GARDEN OF DON JOSE
  Rose Burghley
- [ ] 936 TIGER HALL
  Esther Wyndham
- [ ] 974 NIGHT OF THE HURRICANE
  Andrea Blake
- [ ] 984 ISLAND IN THE DAWN
  Averil Ives
- [ ] 988 THE PRIMROSE BRIDE
  Kathryn Blair
- [ ] 1103 HEART OF GOLD
  Marjorie Moore

- [ ] 1120 HEART IN HAND
  Margaret Malcolm
- [ ] 1122 WHISTLE AND I'LL COME
  Flora Kidd
- [ ] 1124 THE NEW ZEALANDER
  Joyce Dingwell
- [ ] 1150 THE BRIDE OF MINGALAY
  Jean S. Macleod
- [ ] 1167 DEAR BARBARIAN
  Janice Gray
- [ ] 1170 RED LOTUS
  Catherine Airlie
- [ ] 1180 ROSE OF THE DESERT
  Roumelia Lane
- [ ] 1190 THE SHADOW AND THE SUN
  Amanda Doyle
- [ ] 1200 SATIN FOR THE BRIDE
  Kate Starr
- [ ] 1216 ORANGES AND LEMONS
  Isobel Chace
- [ ] 1218 BEGGARS MAY SING
  Sara Seale
- [ ] 1220 ISLE OF THE HUMMINGBIRD
  Juliet Armstrong
- [ ] 1278 THE KING OF THE CASTLE
  Anita Charles
- [ ] 1301 HOTEL BY THE LOCH
  Iris Danbury

**To: HARLEQUIN READER SERVICE, Dept. N 406
M.P.O. Box 707, Niagara Falls, N.Y. 14302
Canadian address: Stratford, Ont., Canada**

- [ ] Please send me the free Harlequin Romance Catalogue.
- [ ] Please send me the titles checked.

I enclose $_____ (No C.O.D.'s). All books are
60c each. To help defray postage and handling cost,
please add 25c.

Name _____

Address _____

City/Town _____

State/Prov. _____ Zip _____

Have You Missed Any of These Harlequin Romances?

All books are 60c. Please use the handy order coupon.